'Ho! says Proust, the novel is akin to the cracked looking-glass of a servant. With the art to be judged, *mes bons amis*, by the quality of the mirror, not of the life. And while that may be true, I think it's fair to hazard a guess that Proust, upon experiencing these fine and invigorating stories of the illustrious Robert Sheehan, who needs no introduction to the world, might find himself compelled to observe that art can be also a whacked-out kaleidoscopic miasma of delightful abandon and fun, as evidenced in this collection, written in locations all over the world, which on completion leaves the reader (and, *je suis certainement*, M. Proust) amused, exhilarated and really quite delighted by the advent of this new and compelling voice into the world of smashed-up mirrors and kaleidoscopes that is literature. You've seen Sheehan act – now watch him dazzle.' **Patrick McCabe**

'Robert Sheehan's writing debut offers a dazzlingly eclectic collection of short stories. Witty, erudite, sometimes perplexing, occasionally confronting, always engaging. Just like the man himself.' **Ben Elton**

'Loving it. Lots of great stories and voices. Not stylistically similar, but the energy or impulse behind them reminded me of Irvine Welsh's short stories – a kind of inclusive curiosity applied to some *what the fuck?* subjects.' **Frankie Boyle**

WARNING:
CONTAINS ADULT CONTENT

Disappearing Act

ROBERT SHEEHAN

Disappearing Act

A Host of Other Characters in 16 Short Stories

Gill Books

Gill Books
Hume Avenue
Park West
Dublin 12
www.gillbooks.ie

Gill Books is an imprint of M.H. Gill and Co.

© Robert Sheehan 2021

978 07171 89700

Designed by iota (www.iota-books.ie)
Edited by Emma Dunne

Printed and bound in Great Britain
by Clays Ltd, Elcograf S.p.A.

This book is typeset in Electra.

*The paper used in this book comes from the
wood pulp of managed forests. For every tree
felled, at least one tree is planted, thereby
renewing natural resources.*

5 4 3 2

To my dad, Joe –
a wealth of songs and poems

Contents

INTRODUCTION

EXT. PLANET EARTH – DAY

Book dun. Intro ... hmmm. Ought to be brief. Somewhat preparatory for the Reader. Ought to retro-actively intellectualise the thing, but in a not-too-direct way. More sideways, so as not to come off all whatever.

Ooh, it's one of those little stop-motion jumping spiders on my tabletop. He swivels so fast my eye can't even see it. He's darting right over to me. He's tiny but top-heavy. And stripy. Now he's on my empty plate. I doubt he eats beets. I wonder if he eats for the same reason as me, to cling to a dwindling sense of immortality?

Ahem ... excuse me.

Dear Reader,

Do you sometimes talk to yourself inside your head? I sure do! Oh … too direct.

I mean, God … am I even supposed to be writing my own intro? Isn't this a dreadful missed opportunity by the publishers to relieve my workload *and* win me some classy author association cred?

Sometimes I catch myself wondering, do we create the stories we tell ourselves inside our heads, or do they create us? And all our hopes and dreams along the way, our beliefs, our thoughts, our minds (little deputy editors) in our heads, which are on our bodies. And why do we regard all of these things in the possessive? Like 'our' handbags. I've always been into films where it's more character-led, like where the protagonist leads with a personal decision, which in turn carries the story along. Duh – I'm the actor.

This book is mostly characters who demanded to be written from the perspectives of themselves. As they stagger through baffling clouds of self-talk. Through their fussy deputy editors' never-ending demands for attention, they unwittingly lay bare their beliefs, which reveal and shape their strange 'realities'.

Other times I wonder, is this human experience of ours about comprehending the mercurial forces that exist on both sides – the immaterial (the indoor stuff) and material (out there, the world)? And, once understood, is it about curating the ideas that get to make the passage across and become action? Are we just border patrol agents, who get to dictate which forces express themselves in the physical world? And ultimately, do those refusals and admissions make up the contents of our 'Character'? But who/what is making the selections? I wonder is this human experience of ours very physical at all. Anyways, I ramble. But screw it, it's my book, and I love a good ramble.

I wish I could remember everything I ever wrote down; I wish I had a photographic memory. Instead of always having to go back through reams and reams and reams of notes, like a crooked old librarian with spectacles on the end of his nose. That's one thing I learned about discovering these characters in the edit. That there's lots to scan. Scroll back, re-read, attach a new note. Cut, remove and remember to re-paste. Jot furiously, here and there, to slot back in for another rescan. Until it's eyelid-heavying and painstaking. And rewarding.

And it really is. To discover these characters through words – instead of the usual gig of embodying them – handing them the reins and letting them determine the direction of their own stories, has given me a deep glow of satisfaction. I'm grateful and proud for having birthed out a book, and for embarking down this road because now writing's become a part of writing me. It has opened in me a more direct portal to that pure creative exhilaration, that fizzy flow, that *Phwoar! Where did I go?* That reckless abandon. That disappearing, if you'll indulge?

I hope you are drawn into their worlds.

Smooch,

Rob

FUNERAL

Written in Barnes, London

MY HAIR IS DONE TO PERFECTION. It took an age to get right down in Kay Flood's salon, but it was worth it. Because at a funeral you want to look your best when you're paying your respects, keep it together at least until the graveyard, and there the wind and the rain can batter you and ruin your hair, and then you can let out the emotions and start crying and all that stuff there too.

I remember Granda Pat's funeral, and Uncle Peadar, who could find no place to belong to other than the farm, turned and goes shtalking away across graves, no respect for the plots or the dead lying in 'em. Just made a beeline, kicking gravel across the graveyard and the wind gusting.

And we all looked and we all looked at each other, a few rolls of the eyes, few nods and eyes down, one or two smirks. He shtalks away and gets as far as the edge of the graveyard that's lined with them big, tall bright-green hedges that was made in a lab, and he unzips himself and starts taking a piss. Then there was a few sniggers. Few tuts. The priest's voice was wobbling – but it had been before, to be honest. My jaw was on the coffin let alone the ground, and my hair was all over the place.

It's disrespectful to wear hats at funerals, unless you're a lady. Or have cancer.

And as well, as soon as you hear about a friend, a dear friend's passing, it's disrespectful to not make that promise to yourself. But here I am in the church at the man's funeral wondering have I really made the promise to myself at all, even though I have a clear memory of making it when I'd heard he died.

And now I'm second-guessing making the promise because I can see the back of her neck. It's behind the two locks of hair, with a ferocious shine off it, on the back of her head, falling down, framing the back of her pale neck, long like a swan's, and me thinking I'm not sure that promise is worth anything now that I'm face to face with the back of her neck. And her short-haired sister holding her round the shoulder in her dark blue.

The promise made inside my head three times in a row was that now that Patrick was dead, I'd never in a million years even think about doing anything with his wife (or widow, now), let alone pursuing her. And, I suppose, thinking the thoughts of the Low Fella that are swimming through my head at the moment is breaking that sacred promise. Damn. Sorry, God, and sorry God for swearing. I'm trying my best.

A promise that had to be made because, in our heart of hearts, everyone here knows that there was always a little glimmer of something between myself and Sinéad. She's such a vibrant woman and I know Patrick was a droll chap – always taking the piss – but you might even go as far as to say sullen on a bad day, with a puss on him like something's just after happening. And they say opposites attract and all that, but sometimes I know she yearned for a bit more energy. Something more than someone hating everything all the time. Taking and never giving anything back, being sarcastic about things and getting his kick that way. I mean, she's a liver! Oh, Christ … What am I thinking at the man's funeral – for Christ's sake, Liam! Well, I suppose it's not a terrible sin to say a man is a dier shortly after he's passed … But it is a sin, Liam, because you were thinking it about him while he was very much alive. No, she was great for him. And I always thought that. Without her drumming a bit of life into him he might have gone more withdrawn. And fellas with that seed who stay alone go that way, especially in a small town.

When she's not cutting hair, she's always raising money for charity and organising things to happen on a weekend on the green. She'd go around with far less airs and graces than she's due.

And that promise can't be unmade so I'm going to help her out what way I can and continue to admire her from afar, and thank God that I'm lucky enough to get that gift.

We do have great goss down in Kay's. Some days I put my hands up on the counter and she plays the backs of my fingers like a piano, before doing our traditional 'cheers'ing with our mugs of tea.

We crossed paths a couple days ago coming down the main street, and in my best serious voice I asked Sinéad who was to do the honours of saying Patrick's Mass, and she said she'd sooner put him in the Protestant church across the road if it wasn't Looney, 'cos the other, newer parish fella has a bit of a reputation. Word followed him from his last place. But there was none of that carry-on in mine and Patrick's time, mind, when we were altar boys. And if there was, I was never told.

Well … if I'm being totally honest, not all of me made the promise. I made it, but not all of me made it. The bit of me that makes all the right decisions, that fella made it. You know this, God. You know the fella who at the end of the night when someone says, 'We'll walk up the road to Doheny's, sure they're open till half two,' and the *other* fella is telling you, 'Go, go, go on, there'll be craic!' That fella who's in the front seat is shouting, being barely heard, 'You've been up to Doheny's a thousand times and it's always the exact same craic – don't bother.' But the booze tends to quieten him down no matter how high-pitched he screams. The booze puts him on mute. But he's the fella I should be listening to, because he's looking out for not only you and me but everyone else around as well. He's got everyone covered.

'Cos no woman wants you smelly and hungover on a Sunday morning. They want the whole family to go out on a horse ride or a drive to the beach and be able to dive into the sea and be all full of energy and not sipping Lucozade and panting, even though you're not moving anywhere, and stinking. No one wants that on a Sunday.

So he's the fella to listen to, the Big Fella. The fella who has your voice, God. He's the one who made the promise. He made it as defence against the *other* fella. He's the one who wants everything now now now. Next week won't do. He wants to taste the forbidden fruit – he's the Low Fella. He's the snake. He's the Devil. And he tempts and he tempts and he tempts. And God knows he likes the drink as well. Because the drink turns up his volume. And down the other fella's.

Anyway, I'm of an age now where I don't listen to that Low Fella as much any more – ah, he's getting to be less tempting these days. So it's going to be easier to believe in the Big Fella up in the front seat, as long as I keep fairly clear of Sinéad – apart from the bimonthly cut and blow dry – and not be thinking about inviting her round all the time. Well, apart from the odd few times after the funeral and she alone in the house. I can invite her all I want around that time, because what kind of devil would I be if I made a problem for her having some company? Poor thing. Must be shocking to lose a partner like that.

Although the amount of energy your man expended, I doubt she's even noticed – haha!

Ah, for God's sake stop it, Liam, bless us and save us you're at the man's funeral.

We were altar boys up there when we were lads. We'd be sniggering away behind Father Looney Tunes. Little boy racers running around, tripping each other up the aisle. Soon as Mam had the car pulled in next to Looney's orangey-brown Capri, the doors would fly open and it was first to the altar, first to the vestry, first to get the albs tied on, first position for Mass. First first first first first. Everything was competition for Patrick. He'd endless energy back in those days but I was never that far behind, always a close second. And he wasn't unkind, but if he ever said a kind thing, he'd a knack for making it sound like a judgement on someone else.

Still though, to this day, when I walk into church every Sunday I get a mad time warp back to when I was a little fella with Patrick and me and a few of the other lads and one or two from the choir. The old frank-incense drenched into the walls for years, centuries. Smell of Old Belief. Was like it was yesterday. And I'm up there lighting candles and ringing bells and trying not to laugh. And so's he.

But he's gone now. He's gone and he'd like her to be happy, wouldn't he?

Now that's arrogance, Liam. God, who am I to say that I could be the one to make her happy? Christ, oh sorry, crikey. Imagine the town goss! Ha. Jesus forgive me and he barely cold. Leaving his children half-orphans, they'd say. Walking across town and into the bed of another man. You can nearly see her house from his. The cheek of it. Would he be as quick to rob his grave?

Uproar. It's almost funny to think about. Ha, the shock on these poor auld bored God-botherers' faces. 'Yeah but, Liam,' says the front seat fella, 'it'd stop being funny after about three days, and then God only knows how long they'd punish us for.' Or if they'd ever forgive us.

And I know she would come too. The two of us doing the eejit up in Doheny's at all hours. I said, 'Sinéad, you'll have another one, sure – you're a liver!' She says, 'I won't have a liver in the morning if I don't go now.' And the two of us would laugh. I remember one night I got a fair laugh out of her. We were talking about Patrick and, now, Patrick would be stocky, solid. There was talk of the county-level team there for a while. And she was rolling her eyes about him being cranky and this and that and whatever and, what was the line I said? 'Well, Sinéad, it doesn't help to be short with people, but then again, some of us can't help it!'

Well. It was the proudest I'd say I've ever felt. It didn't matter that she spat half her pint over me. I got a laugh out of her I'd say I hadn't heard before or since. I wonder did Patrick ever get that class of laugh out of her? Now stop that, Liam. God, you're at the man's funeral.

But the way me and her's eyes have lingered at all hours of the night out in the smoking area after Doheny closed his doors. A man knows. I saw the willingness in her eyes, with them gorgeous dark lashes lingering two, three, four seconds sometimes *without* breaking contact? That's a clear and steady signal.

Beautiful eyes she has too. Sort of piercing grey–blue, like an Arctic wolf.

The bells ring anyway and Patrick gets lugged up on six lads' shoulders – some family, some Patrick used to play football with – and he begins making his way out of the church. The shine off his coffin would make you think it's unnatural, unfit for going into the ground – the gleam of gold on the handles. I wonder how long it will take the worms to eat through the varnish. When I go, I'll be buried in something way less boasty. I've little attachment to the body, the auld cement mixer having to be lugged around. Once I go, the sooner the worms get in at me the better.

As Patrick shnakes down the aisle step by step, Sinéad's head turns with him and the skin on her neck twists then hides behind her deep-brown-coloured hair, and I see those eyes and they're all glassy with tears, and her nose is red and her lips are pursed and sealed and she looks tired, God bless her.

I want to get up and go over and put my arms around her. I want to catch her; and she'd fall into my warmth. I want her to soak my collar in tears. I just want to walk her home after this and gently undress her while she cries and cries and let her curl up in a ball against me just wearing a slip and cry Patrick out and go to sleep. And as she dozes off I'd hug her close and make my breath close-sounding by her ear and make it sound to her like the coming and going of the sea.

Patrick draws closer, slowly making his way down the aisle for the last time, like a twelve-legged caterpillar in his Sunday shoes. Trip the caterpillar for the craic! I am in as much disbelief as everyone else in the church when the Low Fella sticks the left foot out and trips the first GAA fella on the left carrying the coffin.

The whole lot of them go down like dominoes. Hard.

The coffin bounces off the back of the pew in front of me and falls back into the aisle. Patrick's corpse comes flying out and rolls like a crash dummy, landing face up, eyes wide open, staring up at the Heaven he was scheduled to be arriving at in about half an hour.

Shrieks and cries and screams ring out and echo through the church now like hysterical prayer. I can't move in the pew. I'm frozen to the spot. I look up and Sinéad's crystal eyes are ablaze and burning a hole in mine. She points and screeches, 'He tripped him! I saw him! Liam?!'

Everyone looks at me in complete amazement. And suddenly I realise I'm smiling. I'm wrinkling my mouth. I'm trying not to laugh. I get up and try to encourage the lads to help me put Patrick back in his coffin but the football lads all ward me away with thick welty hands on long arms connected to fair shoulders.

This one, a blond curly lad who's rumoured to be a bit AC/DC, probably only trying to cop a cheeky feel here in God's house where no one would suspect, force-whispers at me, 'Go – now,' and gives me a look like he's going to knock my teeth out. I've seen that look in his eye before but only from the sidelines of a match.

I turn around, having finally managed to stop smirking. I can't look at anyone in the face and most of them can't look at me. But a few of them can as I'm walking down the aisle, and that fella in the front seat is roaring in my head, saying that Patrick was a well-liked man, and there are a few lads in this church whose lips are curling, sizing me up, and are going to bide their time until they get a chance at taking a crack at me. A few there slobbering at the thought of giving me a justified hammering.

Oh, jaysus, what have I done …

I'll never live this down. Maybe some people will think it's funny and they'll become my new friends and it'll split the town in two. People who found it a bit comical in hindsight and there was no harm done really and we can all move on and laugh about it, and then the begrudgers who think it's an offence against God, spoiling another man's burial because you were jealous of him and the fact that he got to be with her and everyone knows it, and they all know that's why you did it – for God's sake, will you be quiet? – and would never forgive me. Who knows what's going to happen? Young Willy Boland near the back has a big grin on him. He's had that big pink scar running down from his left eye since before he was eighteen. He's been in the wars well enough. He knows what I'm in for.

Then I'm in tears and I can taste the salt, and I'm heading out the front doors of the church into the light, blinking. I hope to God no one saw me crying on top of everything else.

I'm stood in the car park, unsure whether I should get in my car and drive up to the graveyard, or get in my car and drive home, or wait until she comes out and fall at her feet, like Mary Magdalene at Jesus's feet but in reverse, and beg for forgiveness.

I choose the third option. I stand in the car park making funny noises at the back of my throat and wiping my eyes until the procession have gotten themselves back together and are coming out of the church. The sun is glaring and the wind is up, just my luck.

As the wind gusts them going down the steps, I kneel at the bottom and pray in a forced whisper, 'May Patrick go to Heaven. May Patrick Cleere go to Heaven. Please God, may Patrick Cleere go to Heaven. May Patrick …' My hair has been turned upside down and I look like a complete fucking eejit. And people are hollering and roaring, 'Fuck off, Liam!' 'Go home, Liam!' 'No respect!' All I want to do is tell her but I can't be heard over the congregation of screaming mourners, so I jump up and down and wave. 'Sinéad! Sinéad!' But she's turned away, her head's buried in her lesbian sister's navy-blue blazer, and she's quickly being helped in the passenger door of her car. Volkswagen Golf GTI, sporty little motor. I love seeing her drive through town in that car.

Or see her pull up outside Kay Flood's for our appointment for a blow dry and fizz, and I'd say, 'Well, Sinéad, sink still broke?' And she'd give me the eyes and say, 'Now, Liam, the thing about being married to a builder is he *knows* he can fix it, that's why nothing ever gets fixed!' And I'd roll my eyes and try and keep from letting it out, the knowing that she's going to be giving me the shivers, through my whole body from the top down, when she's giving me the shampoo-conditioner under the hot jets, and beaming, smiling at me and asking is there anything in the magazine.

No sooner does her sister get her sat into her car than she pops back out and comes marching over. I crawl to her high-heeled feet like Mary Magdalene, and she grabs a firm hold of me under my sodden, pathetic chin. 'You are in my prayers, Liam. But you do not have me. You never, ever will. Please do not come to the salon again.'

And she's gone. I try pushing my way through the legs of all the blocking throng to follow her black suede stilettos, but a teenage-Patrick-lookalike pallbearer jumps at his chance. He grabs hold of me by the scruff of the collar. He gets me by my tie knot and is doing that thing where a lad tries to choke you to death with your own tie.

And I can't get the words out, and all I want to tell her is that I love her and that she has a place to stay and someone to talk to if she's feeling lonely, but this little bastard is choking my air passages, so I knock him off and connect fair well with his ear, but he's only sixteen or seventeen and that doesn't go down at all well.

And now the GAA lads have Patrick put into the hearse and three of them are coming for me. I turn to run but I slip on my shoelaces that teenage Patrick must've stood on, and I half trip over but just about manage to regain my footing before the blondy curly footballer fella, I think his name is Cronin – his father was a footballer as well – turns me around and smacks me so hard in the mouth my vision goes completely black. And I feel the contact but not the pain of the massive *thud* on the back right of my head as I hit the cold gravelly ground. Hard. Grinning Willy Boland, who's wearing them New Rock boots that go all the way up to the knee, wades in with a fair kick to my ribs before getting pulled away.

And then they're hoisting me up by the scruff and they look alarmed. There must be a load of blood. Their eyes are bulging and their talk is drifting in and out of my ears. I can't hear properly. God forgive me, I don't want to die, but on the upside … If you die in a churchyard, you're guaranteed entry into Heaven, I'd say. Is that right, God? It's not written down anywhere but why else would all the priests and Protestant vicars bury themselves on the church grounds? It's hallowed, sacred ground, and I think that means I'd get a pass.

The lads have me upright now and are dragging me towards one of their cars – an Audi A3 hatchback, nice motor, one of them hybrids that uses hardly any petrol – so I flop out of their rough grip onto the ground and fake a seizure. I mean … Forecast is pretty grim. Outlook not very bright, really. Becoming the town pariah or, worse, the town joke. Even worse than life now, and that's a rung below I didn't think was down there. And even worse than that, seeing her driving through town or walking little doggy Daisy in those tight jogging pants that highlight how impressively back in shape she got after having three children, and her walking on with the head down and having no wave or smile for me? Her averting her eyes from the low freak, pretending I don't exist? That's an agony worse than an eternity in hell, God. Or a loony bin. No, thank you. Churchyard fix, please.

The second time I go down I go down for the seizure, and this time I feel the full contact and the full pain. I can feel hot blood drenching the back of my head. My hair is in such an absolute mess I don't want to even think about it.

They're all getting the phones out.

You know, I was only thinking earlier on that as you get older the outside world shrinks and shrinks. And things right in front of you get kind of big.

As they hoist me up on the gurney, I can't move a muscle to turn my head away from the spot where Mammy used to drop the two of us off for rehearsals. Next to Looney's Capri, an old motor, with the 'r' and the 'i' prised off the back of it so it just said 'Cap'. Patrick eyeing me with divilment. The seatbelt strap going tight over my chest, making my breathing shallow, like it went having to race him all the time. I hated the feeling of it. It was always first this, first that. And this was before Sinéad knew either of us. First one to reach the altar. Soon as the handbrake was on we were out of the car, elbowing and pulling. Into the church and up the aisle, slapping all the pews and making them echo.

Well, I suppose you won this round too, Patrick. Well done, again. But I was never very far behind.

ENGLISH DEF

Written in the changing rooms
of the gym off Brick Lane

I ASK A FELLA for some help down Brick Lane, and as a way of showing me he doesn't have any money he holds up both his palms. Up in front of him like the hokey-cokey. Like that's a universal sign that someone doesn't have money? I'm not a literalist, but I feel like shouting at him, People usually keep their cash in their pockets not on the palms of their hands, you CANT!

But I'm weak from no grub and Derek's had me up on a pile of party favours the night before, and I don't want to risk getting a box in the head. That's the worst of it. I'm twice, three times the intellect of most of these hamsters, these snappily dressed sleepwalkers, these exciting up-and-comers.

I shout after the lad just to antagonise him the right amount. 'Cam on, mate, it's me birffdaayyyyy.' (It isn't.)

See if that stirs anything approximate to compassion in him, because you know what birthdays mean, don't you? Def. The sanitisation of which has led to an exponential increase in hedonistic binge-drinking culture in this country. You hide away all the bodies, you oblige everybody to give it the *waa waa* and the waterworks, you industrialise it to the point where it becomes a faux pawww, as the Belgians might say, *not* to sell Grandad's corpse back to you. Make it something people daren't speak out about for fear of being called morbid, and only one thing's gonna happen. The one day a year people is celebrating the beginning, and therefore the end, of their lives, they can't cope, so they drink themselves numb under the banner of merriment.

Aaaw! It's only once a year – we might as well let our hair down, eh! What total bollocks people feed themselves. Yes indeed, my people get very acclimatised to the diet of bollocks. Three helpings a day and two Roman-esque feasts a year – one on their birthday, one on Christmas with a cherry on top. Roman-esque to the point of puking but they can't afford the vomitorium so they make use of my Manor instead, and I'm the one that's slovenly? Well, no Roman-esque for me, not me. When dirty death and I lock horns, it's gonna be a head-on fucking collision.

My nearest and dearest comrades are under strict instruction to exhibit my corpse in the most public spot possible for as long as possible. Exhibit me, like I'm dishing out my sermon atop the holy mountain, until the Old Blue bumble along and spoil the fun.

That's *if* my close compatriots don't go first. Derek's been looking a bit green around the gills since he got that hole in his foot that won't close. He limps across Whitechapel Row to the hospital and gets it cleaned but they won't give him shoes, so it just gets filthy again in half an hour. What's the point of that? I laugh at him every time – I says, Every time you come back from there you look *more* like the Elephant Man, not less! The health system in this country, it embraces you with one hand and strangulates you and stabs you repeatedly in the guts with the other, like freaky fucked-up Ganesha on his lunch break. They fuck you up then they fuck you down, about six foot. Or until the fight leaks out of ya.

I told my dear friends approximate that when I eventually kick the bucket after I buckle my last vein, I want to be dragged out by the feet onto Brick Lane in the dead of night and propped against the wall. Pull out my tongue and fashion my face into a big shit-eating grin. Stick a piece of wood in there if necessary. Find a scrap of cardboard, nick a marker and write on it in big letters:

It's My Def Day!

And get as much of the 'Happy Birthday' lyrics on there but replace the word *birf* with *def*. Fuck it, they're the same fucking thing anyway – people will hardly notice.

Next step, Derek's got to fox as many passing punters as he can into taking a picture with my beaming corpse by making a laugh out of it, by saying, Look look

– happy def day! He's not *actually* dead, mind, he just knows that he's definitely gonna die on this day in the future, so he's practising!

Don't wanna freak 'em out too much. Wanna pull the wool well and truly over their already myopic eyes. See how many idiots we can get snapping selfies of my grinning corpse and get them posted on Instagram. Aha, maybe we can set my corpse up on Instagram and get it a little @ symbol. We'll stick a few photos on there and show the eejits, tell them to tag me from the other side ahaaa, yeah!

My dirty, filthy, foul-smelling, smiling corpse will go viral. I'll put my house on it. Who wants to live as a fat, gouty cunt at def's door? I am gonna smash down def's door with a fucking battering ram. Call me Doctor Def Rattle, call me the Grim Reaper Sleepaa.

Aaaaah, yes, I can see it now. My remains pulling a fast one on Brick Lane. They'll call me the greatest exponent of postmodern art since Marcel Duchamp took a piss in Whitechapel Gallery or whatever. Blogs and forums and bullshit like that will pick up on me. Then I'll make the news – I might even make the *Evening Standard* if they can find an angle to use it to vilify us even more, and I'm sure they won't have too much of a problem. Fucking Tory cunts. They think they're clever but it ain't clever to win at a rigged game. I'm telling you, man. It's clever to win when the odds are stacked entirely against you. My intellect is far superior than most of them hamsters. Them pasty, malnourished-looking cunts that sit in the cabinet and never smile. It's like they was told in boarding school that if you smile it's likely to land you a bumming, and deservedly too, so keep your teeth to yourself or the rugby field where you can display them in aggression.

Not me, though – three teeth left standing, and God knows they're on the way out. I display 'em proudly to the world. Well, the world of Brick Lane. Try in vain to wipe the sour-cunt look off these miserable middle-class cunts' faces. And every now and again it works, once in a blue moon – usually with a young lady – and when that happens, it makes my day. It's all I need. No need for food, one can move straight to the Bacchanalian reverie. 'Cos the positive light of the universe fills my belly, no need for toast with jelly, straight to the abyss with a smile on my face. I am all-powerful and have been since day dot, since I learned to thrive on nothing. Next to nothing at all. I'd go a week on a bowl of mashed potato, no botha.

Ahaa! Where's that cunt who ignored me with the palms of his hands? I'm gonna chase him down. Think he cut right on Buxton St. If I cut through Allen Gardens, I can cut him off and give him back the palms. Give him the backs of 'em too. Give him reason to hit me a few good slaps – he'd only be doing me a big fat favour! The more mashed the merrier. Mashed like Mum making potatoes after she'd finished drifting in and was about to drift back out. It was the only thing she could cook that didn't go in her vein, the silly cow. I wish I still had the kiddies and grandkiddies around. I'd teach 'em how to make my mummy's mashed potatoes.

Nah, fuck that, the world are all my kiddies. All you lucky devils, we're lucky to have ya, and when you see my mashed-up face you'll have learned something.

Life IS SUFFERING! Ahaaa! It's inevitable. You've got no control. Fuck me, I learned that when I was six and I woke up to the sound of a crack addict smashing a hammer off my bedroom door, mouthing how he was gonna kill me and eat my little remains. I just stood up on my Batman bedspread and started singing. 'Ha-haaaa,' I said in my bestest operatic voice, 'there'll always be an England, and England shall be free, and if you try and kill and eat me I'll take that hammer and bust it into your addled skull, son, bring it on! You're child's play, I'm the predator, you're the prey. You can't touch me, nothing can. Not even SUFFERING!'

You see, you'll all see when you see my big smiling cadaver. Yes, indeed. For you, I will become the face of English Def. God knows she needs a face, she's been faceless for so long. When you become a corpse, they whisk you away and stick you on ice for six weeks before sticking you in the queue for the incinerator, evil fire-starter, dirty pyro wanker! How fitting for the end of an English life, queueing. Like all you Saturday twats lining up to buy your parents' clothes.

Uh oh, it's the bumbling Old Blue. What? You don't like my sermon? Maybe if you sat back and tried learning something you'd learn something. Give me a beat, give me a beat, give me one of them beatboxes, all speeches work better with a beat behind them! Ut-ss, ut-ss – come on, join in, copper. You must have a talent or two beyond being a thinkless drone.

Oh, fuck off, what do you think handcuffing me is gonna do? You ain't invented a handcuff for the mouth yet, though I bet one day you'll manage, you Nazi cunts. My intellect is superior. You think with an intellect like mine I could've stood doing your job? No way in this hell, sir. My brain would've melted out my mouth long ago, along with my teeth! You know your little metropolitan uniform and your little metropolitan van and your little metropolitan pal there, you know what they tell me? That you're thick! And it's the only job a state that hates you can be bothered to find for you. Bothering people like me who are changing the world, bothering people who can see into the future. I bet you've never even followed your fingernails down to the cuticles, you fucking dullard CANT. Oops, there goes my big mouth – it opens up and shit flies out!

C'mon, you're nothing you are, you're just a uniform. You're a mannequin in one of these vintage shop windows. Put me in your ickle van if you like, tsss – OOOOOWWW, easy, mate! But I guarantee you, sir, you'll be back here in this spot scraping my corpse off the pavement within the month, everything going to plan. I'll stake my fortune on it, within the month.

And then you'll be famous for being the dullard copper who tried to scrape my remains off the pavement, and people will try and stop you, and they'll cuff *your* hands, and they'll start a riot because my stinking corpse will have become their great Monument of

Death. Like Brahma reborn down Brick Lane. I will be at the centre of my own sacrifice. I'll be giving these poor souls back their natural rite. And when you try and take away these Awakened's deity, they will turn on you with a mighty wrath, you see, and tear you to shreds, my poor sleeping son.

So come on, my Old Blue dear, do what you want to me, do it hard and do it angry. Do it ten times over because the more you do it, the more you do to end all these poor people's pain!

My genius multiplied by your stupidity might just overturn this country, England, and together we will end all suffering. We might just lift the two-thousand-year fog. Judging by the blankness on your boat, this might be crazy enough to work.

Gimme a beat! Gimme a beat! Techno techno techno!

Fuck the Queen, fuck the Queen, fuck the Queeeeeeeen.

ROSE

Written on a boat to Nusa Penida, Indonesia

I'M RAPPELLING DOWN the stem of a rose, that sways alone in Chalice Valley.

It took us four weeks to get to her summit, edging our way ever closer to the tippity-top of the flower, moving slowly, slowly, ever cautious of the vast crevasses between the petals. Climbers can plot routes and hack away the thorns, but they sprout back twicc as fast.

Camping on a one-eighty-degree gradient, exhaustively checking and double-checking our supplies are properly harnessed before finally falling into a deep and well-deserved sleep. A sleep that's haunted by giant bumblebees coming in the night to pollinate the flower, but then waking and giggling to one another about how silly it is because giant bumblebees don't go near roses. That's why it's possible to climb them.

Now, our ropes are fastened to the node beneath where her petals bloom. We four are tied together, our fates are tied together, her deep aroma has finally subsided, a little, after four weeks in close proximity.

The trick, when rappelling down the stem, is to time perfectly when you pass the thorns. In prep for the climb, we were warned time and time again about teams who decided they'd gotten into a rhythmic rappel and went too quickly, and were impaled unceremoniously on a thorn that seemed to leap out of nowhere. They come up fast.

Roger, who belays rope in second above, missed the Kiss by an inch about an hour ago. It's given him a real adrenaline buzz; he keeps whooping annoyingly every two minutes. Hollering, 'Woohoo! Makin' pearls!' He frays my ropes. I assured the others he's safe, when you know how to rein him in. He responds to a certain tone of voice.

We were told if it does happen, there's nothing anyone can do but deharness you from the rope and say their goodbyes. You are pinned there, cursed to await your passing, cursed to hear your friends continue on with your expedition while you grit your teeth and see the last of your life through, and enjoy the view from that high up, I guess.

The Kiss. It's not a pretty way to go, but the fact that it is a way to go is part of the reason why we're up here.

Like Minnie's got to relearn since she fell, now that she hates our old oak in the front yard for its weakest branch. We climbed up again and carved our initials into the bark at its highest junction. To steady her, I whispered in her ear that the world doesn't get to live our lives for us, it's the other way around. Shh! It's a secret, don't tell. But she whimpered and sobbed and couldn't help looking down. Somehow, it's only been Roger who can truly lift her spirits.

Red Minnie. Sweet Minnie. Minnie of all my days. A guilt rises in me like the wind off the flats for having barely spared a waking thought for her all through our ascent. Even at Rose's Summit, where we locked arms and held on to each other and gazed for an age out over Chalice Valley.

Roger kept a rare silence, unlike usual when he blabbers on, mouth full of jerky or dried mango.

It's been a long descent, but we're past Half Base Camp on the Lower Stem, and we're so close to home.

Since we were Minnie's size, the air always fit Roger's feet better. He doesn't cope well with the dread of returning to ground. It's that his passion isn't climbing, it's chasing. He's always dangled at the far edge of the branch, which has done me wonders, but he does fray my ropes. I warn him, in one ear and out the other, that rock weakens the nylons, but thorns slash them to ribbons.

To sleep, we anchor down on the jagged green wall and put ourselves back the right way up. Lashing up the portaledges and catching our breath. Peeling off the sodden gloves. We exhaustively check and double-check our ropes to avoid quickdrawing to an unstable node because the piton that's supposed to be there has fallen away. She grows them loose all the time.

We're running on fumes, so instead we chew the fat, Roger mostly. We eat the fruit that Minnie dried. We feel her little hands in the food when we eat it – it's nice. She didn't half mess up the blueberry raisins, though.

As soon as the sun falls behind the western peaks, I am falling into bed. I need my nights peaceful to dream out my days, where Minnie visits in the land of Zs, and we ride on the backs of bumblebees.

Back on the green wall, my team fall back into a rhythmic rappel. We get our blood moving as soon as the sun surpasses the peaks and illuminates the flats below. Just then, a scream from one of our party above. I can't quite make out what's being said because there's a wind hitting the petals above, and they whoosh almost deafeningly sometimes. Must be Roger.

There it goes again: 'Kffdrruuzr! Beeeetlejuice!' What? It definitely doesn't sound like him.

My harness rope has slackened, which means my team have slowed down or stopped somewhere above.

'Kiss from the Rose!' cuts through to my ear.

Oh no …

I'm starting to sweat.

Droplets of blood are splashing onto my helmet. Taking three deep breaths – hooooo, into my feet, hoooooo, hooooooooooooo, OK – I close my eyes and prepare a gory scene in my mind, the goriest I can manage, so that whatever I see up there doesn't hit me as hard.

Few more sharp screams now and I'm turning off my compulsion for revulsion and putting on a brave face, ever cautious that my unknowing doesn't rush my reascent.

When I finally get up to Roger, the others are all hugging him from the sides and bawling from their eyes. You'd think they'd find some decency in themselves not to indulge in their own bullshit while their friend bleeds his last blood. Christ.

I get to his eye level and make safe. He reminds me of a dog I saw when I was seven. We were on the way to bowling in the next town over for my birthday party, and the car in front of us hit this sheepdog. Everybody behind stopped and got out of their cars. I looked down as a pool of blood widened by his panting mouth. I stared at him for a long time, oddly feeling very little. I don't think you have the capacity to feel great sorrow when you're a child. The dog had a brightness in his eyes that I took to mean panic. He looked at me, pleading, and I gave him nothing in return.

I fix Roger with a serious and what I hope is compassionate gaze and shout above the howling wind, 'Roger, I can end it for you right now.'

I take out my large paring knife.

'Just nod your head.'

Whimpers and screams from the others. Gasps of shock as though what I'm doing is crueller than what they're doing, the idiots. They've obviously watched too many bad movies or too much good daytime TV.

'Roger, give me a nod or a shake.'

Tears in Roger's eyes, his and the dog's interchangeable. He wrinkles his lips like he wants a kiss, and forces out the first gasp I'd heard from him since he'd been impaled: 'P-pearls!' He nods.

Through my breath, I find the quiet lapping waves of the faraway Western Ocean in my mind's eye, and the soft skin below Roger's sternum with my blade. I travel it up into his chest and find his heart. I open my eyes. His eyes calm. He stops shaking. I throw my arm across him to feel his passing, to try to sense the wind pass him through me.

His chin falls to his chest and he is gone.

I unfold a large, dried petal that I'd cut for Minnie and wrap it around his body. It'll go some ways to preserving him for a time. Until he's carried away by the birds and re-joins the Chalice. Minnie will be disappointed not to have her trophy, we were planning to carve the Valley scene. But she'll understand in time, I hope.

We reposition and continue our descent, carefully, along her windblown stem.

My mind is racing, I am struggling to maintain the team's steady pace. I can think of nothing now but Minnie. How to tell her? What to say? How do I make her less afraid? How would Roger? How does his Kiss not curse her from forever knowing that the best view comes only after the hardest climb?

We scale down the rest of her jagged stem in silence. Achingly slowly, stained in blood. Whipped and stung by flakes of salt rising off the Chalice Flats. Repentant of our own vainglory, haunted by her piercing, sweet smell. We are so close to home.

SKIN

Written in an Uber in London

I EAT BEHIND MY COMPUTER at lunch now because I've been having dizzy spells. I've had to walk out of meetings, carrying a broken heel. I'm afraid to get up from my desk at work. They're being polite, and not that I care, but everyone must think there's something wrong with me. Our office is open plan. And there's an exercise bike now in the corner office on the floor below. It would be useful to lose a few pounds and save a few dollars, but I can't use it in case I collapse and tear at the hairline cracks and fall out. That would be life-ending, if it happened at work. But if it happened at home, in the mirrors …

After the dizzy spells subside, they leave a severely dry mouth. And a greater and greater feeling of certainty that I am not this thing I claim to be, on the outside. This thing that other people take me for. As far back as I can remember, I did my best to ignore her. I was cause for worry when others caught me flinching at the sight of it. It spoilt the department stores with the festive Christmas décor, catching out someone strange in my reflection.

I've always known and never told. Apart from the Hag. But who in real life could possibly understand? I hate ME in photographs.

When I was seven, I drummed up the courage to practise smiling and looking sad in this antique handheld mirror. The thing staring back was like an instrument I could never quite get the hang of.

Then I was eight, in the attic, when I burnt our first school photo. Me and my brother. Our uniform collars are starched and our hair is overly combed. When he eventually woke up, he cried about the photo. Blubberguts. He couldn't be made to understand what a negative was.

As I lay recovering in hospital, I first had the dream. I was in there much longer than he was and far longer than I should've been because the donor site of my graft got infected and led to hardened swelling. Which meant physical therapy went on forever. That was the Hag's first visit. Or my visit to her, I suppose – whatever. It doesn't matter which one it is. In the dream, I'm always outside her shack, rooted to the spot like a tree. She's always wrapped from head to foot in old rags. I can never tell how bad her leprosy is. I can't see through to the skin under her bandages. But it looks late stage. She revisits as little as once or twice a year, if I'm lucky. I struggle to sleep past six hours because if I relax and just let go, she seizes the opportunity to drag me back there. To deftly remind me to not get too comfortable in my own skin.

The monitor on my desk at work is near the outer edge and faces the wall. Which means I'm out of people's eyeline, away from the central flow. From here, I face the office kitchen. When the coast is clear, I go to the bathroom for checks – combing for cracks, or bulged or burst blood junctions. The bathroom has good low-temperature light. If another girl walks in, I fix my make-up. Hydrating cream foundation with a sheer formula has always been worn.

Though I've had to find a way around it, since I found the folded note left discreetly on my desk: 'It's been noticed that you are spending a concerning amount of time in the bathroom. If there is some medical problem, please seek help, and we will gladly facilitate your time off. Just here to help.' Signed with an X and a drawing of a crude smiling face. I was beside myself. I had to reach for the back of the chair. It was beyond my control to stop the face skin blushing as red as a tomato. Any hotter and it would melt. Now, two pocket mirrors live in my bag and only leave for checks, which have to be done behind my monitor and the contract stack. The most subtle slimline style was ordered. They are frustratingly small.

But I am mostly covered at work. It's just face, neck and occasionally arm skin that I have to worry about.

There is not an otherME working in the same building. But that could change at any time.

Otherwise, I'm just like everybody else. I want what everyone wants – to find love. I went on a dating site. And the guy was OK. Good jawline. Social enough for the two of us. His skin screamed money, but not his own. He took me to a theatre to watch … *Hamlet,* I think? I can't remember. I deleted the experience. The one where the ghost comes in painted sparkly grey and explains how his brother murdered him by dropping poison in his ear. They fanned cold air in to make the scene more ghostly. But it stayed cold for the rest of the three-hour-long show. I shivered and sniffled, it was dreadfully embarrassing. He barely noticed; he was too busy snivelling in tears. They all die at the end? He loved it. No, thank you. Certainly not true-love material. Too many feelings, too much strife: moving on.

If someone ever did come over, I'd have to hide the mirrors. It would be a whole drama. I don't think I could – I don't have that much storage in my condo. But it is a great location, with great lake views between the towers opposite. If someone half-decent ever did express an interest, I'd have no choice but to show him the mirrors. Which would mean concocting some lie that has to stand the test of time. Go down the vanity road? Fat chance. Pretend to be all into dreams and dreamcatchers, and say the mirrors repel bad spirits? There's no way I could sustain that nonsense. Dreams are weirdness. All that loony stuff. Spewing out the day's jargon like a dumpster. They're best left to when you're asleep. And I hate contradiction, but it doesn't count if it happens in a dream. I'm just glad when they fade. They're always gone by the time I'm at my desk in the morning, when I can switch off the Pythons. Who are my *only* waking concession to glee. I'm obsessed. Since even before we moved, they were always on. Echoing down the hallway from the kitchen. I didn't have a clue what they were even saying until sixteen years old.

The home check is carried out in the mirrors, once the whole skin is fully buffed with a pumice under the heat. Time is taken. Every nook probed. Every cranny stretched. Between index finger and thumb, I squeeze my flesh to bulge the skin, checking and double-checking for hairline cracks. With a large tube of surgery-standard skin glue on standby – 'forms an elastic air-tight, liquid-tight seal in just one minute'.

Not that I'd care, but the neighbours think I'm a narcissist. Not the four 'bros' next door; the ones in the two towers opposite facing in. Who see the four standing mirrors in my living room …

But I just shut the curtains. The mirrors are arranged into the portal: two either side in front and two behind, rotated until I'm positioned at the centre of a crowd of strangers who stretch on to infinity.

When I'm nervous, I'm forgetful. When I bought the mirrors, I forgot to scroll down to the bottom of the website to check the specs on what kind of coating sits behind their sheets of glass. The coat that turns glass to looking. What can they see? Are they smooth enough? There's a whole spectrum of specular to diffused light reflection. Either they're perfectly smooth or they're not. Because if not, how honest are they capable of being? and, for now, they're all I have to go on. Their presence maintains vigilance. They're my main line of defence.

I used to despise being naked, for instance. I couldn't even use the word. I had to say 'unrobed' or some other stupid euphemism. But now, I crave it, thanks to them, since I began searching my body.

The problem is, she never told me what it looks like when the search is over. The seams are designed not to be found. If I'm ever to take her advice, then first the main points of umbilical connection – the blood junctions connecting me to the artificial layer – must be found and sealed shut.

At end of day, after my exam and contracts, I am tired. Not to mention up half the night with idiot techno shaking my South of France picture off the wall, if it's past a Wednesday. I like to lay myself out on the carpet floor. My ears go soft and they only listen to the Pythons doing silly voices that don't mean anything. Without them, I'd never sleep.

And later, I enjoy waking up in the mirrors, altogether, when the others are waking up at the same time.

For now, they are my best defence. Along with my peripheral vision. In this city, it's considered rude to look at anyone directly. My peripheral is as good as my central vision, which is an absolute must. Especially as, more and more, I'm at pains to avoid otherMEs. I don't know if our numbers are growing, or if I'm unlucky. Thank the Hag none work in my building, though that could change. But around, in stores and stations, streets and buses … in the same skin. Cross my heart and hope to die. They might have different hairstyles and clothes. But all over, more appear.

I won't catch ME coming when I'm trying to go, because that would mean confrontation. Which means blushing. The second thing I hate most in the whole world. Because it's not *my* skin. But it *is* my blood. That it uses to expose me to others for feeling something that ought to remain private – my business, and no one else's.

In the post-work rush, that hour of the day when everyone is scrambling to get home, I find myself across the street from the office in the queue of the grocery store – only two places behind an otherME. I can't run. I am rooted to the spot. My heart is pounding loud enough that other people can hear. My basket slips and makes a deafening crash. The person in front helps, and the otherME in front of them, their legs move, but I gather everything up lightning fast. I stare at my shoes to try to hide the blushing, until they all turn and face the correct way in the queue and stay put.

Who knows who this other girl is underneath? Or whether she even knows. I've never been permitted to see *my* true face. Who's to say this girl is any different?

If we lock eyes, then what? We're supposed to just have a casual chat? Nope, thank you. Not funny material. She might get upset. Not everyone is awarded the mental integrity to cope with such a heavy load. And people would notice, they'd have no choice.

Through checkout to the exit, I just listen to music, look at my socials and quickly bag my shopping, unable to stop thinking: *So what if it's an otherME?* What good would come from exploring the discovery? Any plans to go public with something like that I would nip in the bud. It would open up a can of worms because once two MEs' photographs were online with the story that we'd never met, tons more would come crawling out of the woodwork. Nope, thank you. I'd rather let them live their own lives.

On the bus home, a man presumed homeless shouts a bunch of mumbo-jumbo at the back. He looks like he smells. Not that I care – I'm nearly home free and can barely hear. The Pythons are up max. Spam, spam, spam, spam, spaaaaaaaaam.

The drunk stands and starts pointing and spitting something about … twins? I remove my headphones. And family ignoring family something, and two some-thing else – pointing and gesturing toward the front. I can see him in that big convex mirror above ME in my periphery. My stomach churns. My stool loosens. The heat rushes to the skin on my face. It's raining, and we are still about a mile from my stop. He is on his feet, holding the vertical rail. I can tell I only have a fraction of a second before he staggers up to me, gets in close spitting vile phlegm, and announces to everyone that my 'twin' has followed me onto the same bus from the store, further down the back, and that I should've seen her, and the fact that we're not sitting together is a sin, and that it's rude for people to ignore each other when it's so obvious they share a mother. Other people don't need that aggravation at the end of the day. They've had enough stress at work. I pull the emergency cord at once. No sillying around. No comedy sketches.

The bus screeches to a halt. I march down the stairwell and leap off. I can hear the bus driver's muffled voice saying something from behind the screen. People stare at me. I see the bum in my periphery, at a safe distance. He's wiped his filthy coat on the condensation and is sticking his mouldy face up against the window. His mouth hangs open as he watches me make my getaway. He waves at me out the open slat as the bus pulls away.

I pray for no dizzy spells, as I shield myself with my briefcase in the rain.

As soon as I'm indoors, I shower immediately. I disappear in the hot steam for a while, and permit the feeling of certainty to slow my beating heart that it isn't ME. Not on the inside. After several rounds of exfoliation, I apply band-aids. Then I go between the mirrors, still wet. They are still in portal position from last night. The light from the traffic below refracts through the sliding door – red, white, then flashing yellow – until I pull my curtains.

And we're all alone. To begin the checks. Starting at the soles of the feet. To the backs of the legs. From the rough heel skin all the way up. To under the armpits. Probing and pulling each small hair, in case it's rooted along a hairline crack.

I can't whistle. I wish I could. But I like to hum along with them under my breath as I work. The

Pythons help to drown out the dumb house and techno rattling down my wall. If I knock, they only turn it up.

Down the backs of the arms, thoroughly pinching and pinkening the skin. Combing carefully over the white scarring of my graft. Looking for any white patches to show inconsistency in blood flow. The base of the skull. Along the hairline. I dig the nails under the chin and work them along the jawline. Behind the ears. Between the toes.

Until sleep takes ...

And I am always reminded of the contradiction, of how I am unable to smell in dreams except when I'm dragged back to her ... I can always smell this familiar air of something, but can never quite place it. It's always just out of reach. The vast flats that surround her waste-ground shack are hemmed in by dark, distant mountains, all tipped with snow. Pint-sized tornadoes leap up and dirty my knees.

As usual, I am powerless to move. Rooted to the ground like a tree. Outside her hut, with its corrugated iron sheet for a roof. A piece of silken red rag flies on a nail.

She is leaning out the wooden shutters of her small window, waving a bandaged hand in my direction. Erratically, like she needs me to come visit with her. Nope, thank you. I refuse. What she refuses to comprehend is that I cannot – I am completely stuck.

I am unable to remember if leprosy is contagious, in the dream. Is it airborne? I don't know – I wouldn't drink her water.

She is shouting but her face is bandaged and her words are muffled. Maybe her tongue has rotted off.

As usual, I can't stop myself. 'Fuck off. Leave me alone!'

The dust kicks up and stings my eyes.

Her shack door creaks open, whining on its hinge. And here she comes … I expect she'll get in close, like always, spitting vile phlegm. My only defence is to fill up my lungs, purse my mouth, hiss the air out slowly and plan for when I awaken, to Google leper colonies, to see if there are any I can afford that look nice. If I sold the condo … Maybe one with a golf course? Or tennis courts? Not that I would use them. I'd be too worried I'd send a finger flying on my backswing. But at least if they had courts it would show that the rest of the resort is of a certain level. I at least want a private room with a bath – I have a shower in my condo. Not a huge amount of storage. I calculate how long, as she draws closer, limping – god, it always takes her forever! – it will take before I'm also a leper and have to start relying on charity. Maybe two years, three max? Depending on how quickly it spreads.

I want to get this over with so we can come to in the mirrors, and I can drink some hot cocoa.

As I feared, the worst happens. She gets right up close in my POV with her bandaged, twisted-up face. The air of something sharp and pungent blows strongly on the wind. It's disinfectant … Coming from her, the Hag. It's floral. Citrussy and summery. What a pleasurable contradiction …

She takes a clean breath in – no wheeze. I wrongly recalled … I can't avoid it, as she leans in whispering, 'My Grrendel.' She calms the dust devils down. Now, I can hear her crystal clear.

'Ewe ore Grrendel. Ewe hov been heeden too long … Da mask hos eaten too much uf de face.'

Her breath smells of phenol.

'Ewe re'ember Grendel. I show hee picture ewe in a book. Many yeares ago. When ewe were young.'

Her rags smell of fresh hospital bedsheets. She taps my temple with a bony finger.

'You hov too be ready for whot ewe look like, underneet. All uf dis time twogather. Ewe and eye. Whot ore ewe now? Twenty-saven. Twenty-saven years, no son. No air, no ahnatheeng … De likelihud ees dat yur skin is suffereeng.'

She clasps and holds my face in her bandaged hands. Her eyes are fiercely hazel.

'Oftair ewe cut yourself awt, oftair ewe peel. Ewe weel see red streaking flies in the darknesssss.'

She hisses me calmer. I am relieved to be rooted to the spot. Otherwise, I would struggle to stay standing.

Her voice becomes lower and full. More melodic than I recall.

'Ofter ewe cut yourself awt, ewe will need to air ouwt. For at least uh manth too seex weeks. Ewe must get time off frum yur wurk. Ewe must discard de skin immediately – owll deese years in de rot like Grendel, in de cave weet no breeathe.'

I stop trying to forget what she's telling me, and listen.

'When ewe locaite de blood connexions, hold on den du gauze. Dey weel stop de bleedeeng.'

I fall into her, but can't fall. All I want is to sit down in her shack and drink a hot cup of cocoa.

'And ewe must stay out uf de sun. Compleetely. Ewe weel feel de cheel, but opain curtin fur torty minutes per daie. De rest of de time? Dark. Nesssss. Otherwhise, ewe weel hov de skin consser foster dan I con cleeck my two gud feengers.'

She snaps her index finger and thumb. The middle one is missing. I wish I could click my fingers.

'Yur feengers weel be yur eyes. Let dey probe ewe, far und wide. Let dey feel ewe. Du bild yur hondskin. Tuff!'

She slaps my palms. Together. A drop of wet beads down my leg.

'Ewe weel know what ewe truly feel laike.'

Oh …

'Ewe weel run yor feengers over yur body anew.'

She has never permitted me to be me. While waking … I'd give anything to feel it.

'When ewe cut yourself awt, t'will make yur legs leep awt your ears! Ewe weel black ouwt. It weel pain, like in hospital. But oftair, ewe weel hold the wrrld in yor honds. And, ewe weel learn blisss. Blisssssss, Grendel.'

She drops away below my POV. Her fragrance hangs in the air – lemon geraniums? No, it's lemon-scented starch solution … The wind calls back the salty dirt. It devils around the front of her shack. Her sheet iron roof rattles. Her old wooden door bangs on its hinge.

I come to in the mirrors, beside myself. The handskin is damp. It's 2.36 a.m. – we were together as long as we always needed to be, six hours.

I can't fully catch my breath. There's this strange thing stirring, under the skin. Like, if my true face was a feeling. I can't stand up and risk a spell, but my heart is beating so fast I have to check my phone.

I quick search 'The Best Mirrors Made Of'. Of course – silver glass is the best. But way out of my price range. And I see why. They're too fancy for this condo.

Another tab springs results out of 'Leprosy Resorts'. Some don't look too bad. They look peaceful. The sun is shining against whitewashed walls in a lot of them. I stream a video of a leper choir singing 'Count Your Blessings' by Johnson Oatman Jr. 'Count your many blessings, name them one by one, and it will surprise you what the Lord hath done.' They're not bad. They make nice harmonies. Their voice boxes clearly haven't rotted away.

The feeling devils around inside me, dizzying my ghost. If I look at it directly, it just dissolves, but if I look at it in my periphery, it turns this vaguely familiar colour. A kind of darkish purply red. I can't place it ... I'm sure I felt it before but it's been forever.

The handskin is slick with sweat opening a new tab to quick search: 'How to Flay a Human Body'.

There it is. Result.

I never made it this far. My head is spinning. I can't stand up for love or money. The feeling shifts and murmurs like a flock of birds. I can sense her. I feel her. In my periphery. Her face is so familiar. It's a face I have met for sure, but can't remember when or where.

Raw-boned cheeks under defiant hazel eyes. Blonde lashes, with little streaks of light red running through them, the tone of a Bengal cat.

Lips are full and dark and have a large, more pronounced Cupid's bow.

My brow has less of a hangover.

My eyebrows are lightly toned but thicker.

My chin is fuller too, with just the smallest hint of a dimple.

My laughter lines sit pleasantly as a natural continuation of the upward curves of the edges of my mouth. My nose is at least a full degree more petite and pointed.

My skin. My skin is still pale, but mottles a light brown in the sun. I see me lying naked and defiant on a beach in the south of … Cuba? Mexico? Florida? Budget depending. Naturalised to the sun, not hiding under a parasol for the first time in my whole life.

She no longer feels out of reach.

Work will be a hurdle; they'll find the new change strange. But in the end, they'll be persuaded to accept a happier, more courageous me. Not ME, who takes incessant bathroom breaks, who induces worry and deserves little more than a note.

Across lots of discussion threads and image boards, I find that the best results for flaying are achieved by hanging the subject upside down. It keeps them conscious and alert, and prevents unnecessary blood loss. I rush down in my robe to retrieve the building's communal ladder, from where I lug it up twelve flights because it won't fit in the elevator, and I nearly collapse from a spell and fall down the stairs.

I pull the wiring out of the ceiling spotlight right above where I sit in the mirror portal. I knot a long red silken scarf to the exposed wiring, one that will hurt the least in taking my weight. I lay some garbage bags out on the floor, for the drops I might miss with the gauze at the umbilical junctions, or in case there's some congealed mess between the real and cosmetic layers. I *have* to know what connects the two. The junctions will expose something godlike. Not one showing … Not a hairline crack in twenty-seven years, and I'd know.

I turn the heat up to seventy-seven.

Most medieval sites say it's best to marinate the skin in boiling water or the hot sun first, but the shower and volcanic pumice are the best I've got. Once it is supple and the body is hung, one cuts to save. It's vital to keep it intact. And who knows, I might want to invite the four neighbour bros over and use it as a tablecloth.

The most common advice states to start just above the knee. Worry about the feet later. Then, the penknife is worked slowly upwards and around with gentle pulling, until all the bonds between the two layers have been severed.

If properly loosened, the leg skin comes off in five or six careful pulls, but I am certain I can get it done in two because I'm my own torturer and the skin is artificial. So the pain, if there is any, will keep me focused.

A trick I read on multiple threads: make a loosening incision along the tops of my shoulders first and around, separating the arms from the torso, before the final pull down. It is a lot of skin. That way, I'm not sillying around like a Python trying to get it over my head. Like a woollen school uniform sweater that shrank to half the size in the tumble dryer. Get a good solid grip around the hanging lip, and wrench the whole thing down. Down, and down quick. The quicker the better. Tear off the band-aid. Whip it off clean and be ready with gauze.

I'm prepared for that stage to hurt a little; it may hurt a lot, but who cares – after will be bliss. And if there's blood, then so be it.

On the floor within reach, I arrange all the vital necessities: skin glue, a bottle of methylated spirits, a bottle of water, plenty of gauze, fresh bandages, Bluetooth speaker remote, aspirin, spare (less sharp) penknife, some tea tree oil I got from secret Santa at work.

And there's my cue. *THUMP, THUMP, THUMP.* Thank you, Hag, for such an encouraging sign. The guys have just stumbled in next door and can always be relied upon to be unneighbourly. They begin blaring their shitty techno, tempting my whole drywall down. I give them the swift knock of faux irritation and, predictable as always, they turn up their volume.

This powerful new feeling unfolds to slow my racing heart, as I climb carefully to the top of the ladder and double knot my ankles with the red silken scarf.

Shame I won't be singing in that choir, but I'll find a non-leper choir. I can't *wait* to see her looking back at me. Will we even need the mirrors around once I'm certain of what I see?

I won't keep the whole skin as a memento, or a tablecloth, not even a picture of it, nothing. Her instructions were clear. It's best completely forgotten. Once it's removed, I will tie it up in the garbage bags and take it out of the city and find somewhere to bury it.

On some hunting threads, I read that when the kill is fresh it can be messy and icky and gross, so make sure you don't lose your nerve halfway through by singing a cheerful song, to keep spirits up.

Pythons at the ready with the speaker remote, humming – 'Hmhmhmhmhm, hmhum.'

My voicebox is wobbling! I kick the ladder out, swinging – 'Hmhmhm … to laugh and smile and sing.'

The techno rattles *THUMP, THUMP*!

Dizzy feeling … Hanging upside down. Head spins. Nausea. Black spots and a severely drying mouth. Red flies are streaking in my sight. And, shit, I left the curtains wide open!

Everybody can see us, all of the people in the towers opposite, see ME hanging naked from the ceiling?!

I clamber up my legs as quick as I can and cut the red scarf above my ankles. I fall in a heap on the floor. Mortified. My head is swimming. I crawl across the floor to get the curtains drawn. I cover my crimson body with a bathrobe. I crack the front door and check the communal hallway to make sure the coast is clear, then return the ladder to its area downstairs – in case anyone should be looking for it – very slowly.

By the time I am climbing into bed, it's already past 4 a.m. That gives me only four more hours until I have to get up for work. Two hours less than the six minimum the Hag needs to pay me a visit. I can learn to live on five hours a night. Lots of people do it.

If I oversleep, and she drags me back, and I have to tell her … She'll be so disappointed. She was so proud that she'd finally gotten through; that I was actually going to go through with it. My head weighs down the white pillow. I am so tired. We are so sick of each other. Since the Hag, life has been a strange dream. One she only drags me out of to remind me that I'm still awake. And not to get too comfortable in this skin.

If she's *that* determined to hold onto her, then fine – she can keep me.

MEDUSA

Started in New Orleans, continued all over

YOU HOPED IT WOULD BE SEXIER.

But when you two get back to her flat that night, she just marches straight in, leaving the front door wide open for you to follow.

Then you're there standing like a spare prick in the middle of her living room, not knowing where to put yourself, while she pads into her kitchenette. 'I'm gasping for a KitKat! I've got sweet teeth.'

'D'you live alone?'

She shouts from the kitchenette like you two are still in the bar. 'Yes, honey, I already told you! Look at my coffee table – it's one of mine …'

You sneak a peek through the open door into her bedroom, which is a mess. Clothes and cups and KitKat wrappers strewn all over the floor. A few empty bottles of Newcastle Brown. On the far side of her bed is some sort of shrine. A large pink embroidered throw thrown over a big stack of shoeboxes, with lots of candles and doilies and giant globs of old, dried wax. At the very top is an ornate gold-framed picture of a woman.

You pray to Jesus it's not a shrine to herself. Rumours have swirled like gusts of wind around Macclesfield of airs and graces, but you're doubtful of the possibility of getting a hard-on, let alone getting over the finish line, if you have to do it next to a shrine of *herself*.

'It's always safer to feed the snakes *before*, you know, anything happens. If we're fortunate, it should knock them right out.'

On closer inspection, you can see that the woman in the shrine is someone other than herself – phew. With fierce-looking dark brown eyes.

It occurs to you to wonder if Medusa doesn't swing both ways.

In the lamplight, something's moving on the shrine next to the picture frame. Lots of somethings, wriggling in a plastic lunchbox …

Medusa pads out of her kitchenette holding her Rasta-style beanie with airholes in her hand and just throws a blindfold at you. No offer of a KitKat, cup of tea, nothing. Instead, she waltzes all blasé past you into her bedroom, takes off her black leather jacket and tosses it on the floor. Like you'd booked in for an appointment or something? Urrrgh.

You follow her into the bedroom and your mind is scurrying like a little mouse, gnawing through thought after thought, and you can't work out whether the woman in that shrine is real or imaginary.

'Who's the lady in the picture then?'

'Oh, her? She whose name we dareth not speak? It's a secret – sssshhh.'

When she shushes, her head snakes go *Hssssss*. She lights some candles. In the dimness, she looks strange kneeling on the bed with no shirt on, still wearing her extra-large, extra-polarised sunglasses. Not sunglasses, more like them retro steampunk goggles that cover the sides of the eyes too. She assured you earlier over shots that the goggle glasses were safe because they let less than half the light in, or something.

'OK,' she says. 'I'll give you a clue. Her name begins with an Aaaaa ...' She leans forward, all faux sexy, with her mouth wide enough open that you can see the back-of-her-throat thing jiggling. 'Now put on your blindfold. Or else.'

'Hang on, two ticks. I just have to pop to the bathroom.'

Behind the dark glasses you see an eyebrow raise, as though she's suspicious of you leaving or something.

'I'll be right back.'

'Go ahead. First on your right.'

In the bathroom, you sit down so your piss is quiet. You piss on the ceramic, so you can listen for her outside the door. You curse her for not having any mirrors anywhere, so you can't even give yourself the once-over before getting down to it.

You tap at the base of your shaft. You decide against doing a little prelim warm-up wank to get the engine ticking before going back in, in case she hears.

Instead, you attempt to conjure up the girls of your past, but all four of them refuse to show. Between all this, and the skinful before, and the condom, you are officially in grave doubt as to whether you'll even be able to get the job done. But from the neck down, she's hot as fuck and well up for it, so … Man up.

Back in her bedroom, and Medusa's naked on all fours. She's gripping the metal bedframe. You take off your shoes and socks. You can barely see the floor for all her crap. The bed is covered in embroidered cushions and pink shawls. A condom sits on the corner.

Her snakes look subdued now – a couple are still awake but woozy. Most of them have knotted themselves asleep beneath her chin.

As you roll on the condom, 'What are those little wriggling things in the box, then?'

Her voice is pure silk now. 'Ah, the *Bombyx mori*. Silk moths. My favourite ickle critters. One more day and they'll be pupating. Oh, honey!'

And you oblige her – phew. You're managing to get things off to an OK start. Doggy style, obviously – safety first. You're determined to get it over the line so that Craig or Kev or any of the other cocks around town can't say that you couldn't save face, because they all saw you leave together. But you hoped it would be sexier … Instead, behind the blindfold, having sex with Medusa is making your head go like a mad hungry mouse, *squeak squeak!* Gnawing through thought after thought after thought after thought.

Like the thought of how her head snakes remind you of your pet snake Eldridge from when you were a kid. That slick dark-and-light-green camouflage look. You got him with your confirmation money, much to your dad's chagrin. Eldridge was a reticulated python who never grew to full size. How proud he'd be of you now if he could see you rocking the worlds of all these cool magic head snakes, having sex with (formerly) the most beautiful woman in all of Athens? Mint. Ravaged by Poseidon, and now you? Phwoooar, come on. That's it. That's what we're talking about, that's it, concentrate. Stay with her, stay with her …

'Honey, such strong hands!'

Squeak! Your head's gone again, to tonight's date in MASH bar, which wasn't too bad, actually – certainly not as bad as anticipated. You'd spent the day's dread at the site imagining worse, but a few swift pints before made ignoring all the sideways looks easier.

You didn't know if anything was going to happen until about half ten, when she snatched your half-drunk pint, necked it and slammed it down, and clasped your hand in hers – first physical contact – and then she made the come-here motion with her index finger, and you got a semi in your blue jeans. She dragged you up from the table while you tried to hide your hard-on. You secretly hoped she noticed.

She danced you onto the student-clad sweating floor and your heart pumped with excitement and promise.

How fit she looked from behind in those tight jeans, for an older bird, even with the airhole beanie on. She *had* to be down the gym toning. You knew it was definitely on when she roared in your ear over the tunes while stroking your earlobe that you don't need your eyes open for good sex. That they're the last place you should be looking.

Now the bed's banging against the wall. 'Oh, baby, that's it. That's it. Yeah, baby, yeah yeah yeah …'

Squeak! On the dance floor, she tickled her fingers across the back of your shoulders, giving you a shiver, which felt good but made you feel embarrassed. And the tipsier she got, the more lopsided her goggles became. And you were trying not to make a big thing of the fact that you'd your eyes pointed squarely at the dance floor, or fully shut, because you were making out that the tunes were so good, that they were keeping you fully engrossed.

Then she cleared the floor of sweating students when the beanie came off and got stuffed in the arse pocket of her jeans. And you would've challenged any man *not* to flinch if nine or ten mini-serpents were giving him their undivided attention.

That's hot, that is. Cheating death all casual and cavalier in a crowded public bar. That's it.

The memory sends a flush surging through you. Hold on to it, you can hold on …

Medusa, white-knuckled, grips a hold of the bedframe. 'Yes, honey, yes. Harder.'

Squeak! Gnawing, gnawing, gnawing and you can't stay in the bedroom, and you couldn't help blushing after the bar staff told her to put her hat back on. Then she necked the last of a double something and tonic and bellowed, 'What do you do again? Oh yeah, building – yeah, you told me.'

At that point, you could barely hear what she was saying, and her head snakes were hissing and snapping at you when you leaned in too close to listen.

'In *training*! Apprentice.'

And she slurred, 'And I'm a cursèd artist. Shhhh, don't tell anyone. And stop flinching, for Jupiter's sake, they don't bite. They might fuss, but that's only because they looove me.'

And as she led you by the hand out of MASH bar, she slung a lazy salute at the bouncer, who gave you a look right in your eyes that carried warning. Walking home, she skipped and staggered in zigzags and spun around on street poles all hyperactive, up to where her eyes used to be in booze and sugar. She spoke too loud on the quiet streets like she was still in the bar.

'… fortunately for you, since the attack, I was left with no choice. Fleeeeee! What else ought a girl to do but seek refuge and try her best to blend in, here in hideous Macclesfield!' She threw her arms up to behold Macclesfield, like she was giving you a guided tour. 'But I like it OK. Good transport links – I'm hopeless at driving. And I feel safe! Here in my lovely little flat, all mine. My little temple. Wait until you see. I have an exceptional view of the old silk factory. I miss that job … Terrible hours, deafening noise.'

She moaned that she missed her sisters, but that the distance they share is good. That she's nearly broke having to buy larger and larger sunglasses to quiet the concerns of her neighbours who, more and more, will leap on any reason to kick off.

She did this fit coquettish twirl near the top of the hill where she threw her arms in the air and kind of thrust her hips out like a belly dancer. 'But I'm pretty fine, though, don't you think?'

That's it! Hold it. That twirl. That 'I am up for it' twirl, right there on the street, where anyone could've seen: that should see you over the finish line. Just don't eye-fuck the poisonous mantelpiece when you're poking the ancient fire.

'Oh yes, baby, yes baby oh baby.'

Squeak! Haha, must remember that one for tomorrow when you're telling Craig and Kev. Poisonous mantelpiece, ancient fire, poisonous mantelpiece, ancient fire.

'Yes, yes, grab me. Yes yes, harder, harder, HARDER!'

So, you dutifully oblige. You can't stop thinking, though, no wonder her neighbours are driven spare. Then, from inside the darkness of the blindfold you hear one snake sick up its supper. *Blaaap.*

You so desperately want to see the sick that you slide the blindfold up a bit, into more of a bandana-biker look. The sick is only small, and it drips down the back of her head and onto her neck and shoulders. Well funny. The snake looks proper shocked by its own sick.

And since you're there, you can't help drinking in an eyeful.

Rumours swirled about how old she was, but no one knows for sure. Apart from the face, age has not taken much of a toll. Supple skin. Hourglass toned. Well fit. You so desperately want to grab her where her hair used to be.

You tease the crease of her spine with your finger and thumb and tickle all the way up to between her shoulder blades, like she did you in the bar.

The snakes rear up and go fierce, hissing and snapping. But you know that they know they don't have the reach. So you flip them the middle one and stick out your tongue. You pull her roughly back by her waist. You are squeezing the cheeks of her perfect ass.

'Oh, baby, you're so strong! I love your hands. That feels so incredible. Please, don't stop. Come on me!'

The bed is slamming. Her body is shivering.

You are the Man. You are Perseus the Godslayer. Wait until they all hear tales of your Odyssey.

'Oh! Oh! Yes honEEEEEEY!'

POP!

The room goes black with coloured spots. You let her fall onto her back as your legs go to jelly, helpless to the ancient rhythms usually restricted for the Godheads.

Hhsssssssss!

Moaning Medusa arches her back, shuddering in pleasure, and whips her head back and catches sight of your blindfold-less eyes out of the corner of hers.

Now, you can't hear her screaming, 'Pull out! Pull out!'

*

Because the last thing you wanted was another stone penis lodged in your vagina. When that happened, you had to call Stheno and Euryale in the middle of the night to help get you to A&E, where you had to have a painful procedure carried out by a surgeon who you thought was too rough, so when he was done and you were given the all clear, you mortified him back for being a clumsy asshole.

It took the Gorgon sisters an age to show up that night, and when they did arrive you were fearing the worst that, yes, you were expected to suffer the Nightlink to get you to the hospital. 'You couldn't spring for a taxi? Why did you come all the way here if it wasn't in a fucking car to pick me up?'

Your sisters cowered and you felt hideous once met with their reply. 'To help!'

You could trace the thought along the bridges of their noses. That the curse didn't change you – you're still the same as you always were.

And then there was that old lady who broke foul wind next to you in the lift and then gave you a look as if to blame *you* for it. She had a big, wide, flat arse, so you sanded her down and laid her on her front as a coffee table.

Stheno suggested afterwards, after you'd calmed down, that she might just have been apologising with her eyes. Or saying 'I have terrible gas'.

You promised them it wouldn't happen again …

Back in your bedroom, you stripped the fitted sheet off the bed and threw it over your man. His erection stuck up in the air like a tent pole.

In your dressing gown, you stepped quietly out onto your balcony walkway. With a cup of coffee, a KitKat and a fag. The morning sky had just begun to grey. From fourteen floors up in the tower block, you got a full view of the old silk factory. Way back in the seventies of the seventeenth, the industry was still just cottage-sized. You, and maybe twenty or thirty other local women and children.

At that time, the hillside was covered in the most beautiful hard-wooded holly trees. Perfect for making button moulds.

Folks paid heed to your glasses and stick and accepted you as blind. Despite that, they kept you on for your tireless hard work. And you got some peace from the loom. Those groaning, deafening machines. You'd work until the throstle felled you to sleep. And you slept until the whistle of the skylark, singing in mid-flight, would wake you up at dawn. And you'd drink some hot coffee and eat some bread with dripping, and get right back to work making bridal buttons and ones for expensive suits. Plenty enough to live on per week – mind, it was six days working – along with a few swiped buttons here and there. But you only swiped ones that reminded you in secret of ones you owned before Athena took your face. The ones that walked the tightrope between orange and red. What was that colour called? Apollo be bound, you've learned its name but have forgotten it so many times! That colour that could transport you back to Athens at the very moment the sun was falling behind the Parthenon, better than all the rest could.

Vermillion! That's it. That's the shade the dawn can turn on a rare morning over Macclesfield.

Back in your room, and Athena's picture got knocked off her shrine. She lay on the floor face down, and her glass was smashed to bits. You picked up your box of *Bombyx mori*. Thank Athena they hadn't fallen out. They were all still alive and wriggling.

You crouched on the bed next to him, your poor man. You held onto your knees, staring at nothing, listening. Listening for any grumbles from next door. Imagining the neighbours waking up, being angry and banging on the wall again. They were driven spare. You wished they would come and complain, but you knew none of them were brave enough to knock on your door and read you the riot act to your face.

You wished you could scream, but tears would have to do. You lay down beside him and cried, and darkened the stone of his face. Not that his orgasm should peak and pass, but out of spite. You deluded yourself into hoping that you petrifacted all your victims to a realm of eternal orgasmic grip. But you know in your heart of hearts that such a place is a Myth and only exists in a pervert's fairy tale.

Your mind is plagued with 'I am a plague, not a priestess'.

Behind the tower block, a few miles along the Bollin River past the reservoir, was a forest where the skylarks could always be heard, singing in mid-flight, at that hour of the morning. You liked it there, you walked there often. Not like that godforsaken little island that the sisters would love to dump you back on for the rest of eternity and forget about you, if they had their way. That was another good thing about Macclesfield, that there was a a good fifty miles between you and the wretched sea.

You were sad to have to leave Macclesfield, but you had no choice.

When that boy didn't show up on the building site next week, they'd come looking. Everybody saw you two at MASH bar together, and everybody saw you leave. It would only be a matter of time. It was a real shame. You'd miss the view ...

The Gorgon sisters would be furious, having to find you somewhere else. Again. You *promised* them after last time, you promised them that things would be different. You promised them that you'd finally found a sanctuary worth holding on to. But you already knew what they would say – that you said that *last* time you lived in Macclesfield.

And you knew what they wouldn't say – that you were an endless burden, and the sole reason that the three of you couldn't live together as a family.

As you scattered a bagful of his stone chippings in the forest, you muttered a prayer of apology under your breath to Athena.

As the *Bombyx mori* wriggled free along the branches and leaves, you begged her for a smooth and peaceful transition to wherever it was you were destined for next, and that the sisters could find a new tenant for the flat quick enough.

You crouched down and drizzled your former lover and his soon-to-be grieving family a small drop of

Newcastle Brown, before necking the rest and slinging the bottle in the weeds. You felt pained to admit to him that the night you two spent together, you felt spaced out, like you weren't really there. You didn't feel fully yourself again until the point he changed.

And as you emptied the dirt out of the plastic lunchbox you thought, 'Maybe I should do the blind lady thing again. Get a seeing-eye dog. You can get a seeing-eye pony these days – that might be fun, give my new neighbours something else to squawk about.' But then, you thought, 'No … The snakes wouldn't like it if I introduce another animal into our situation. They'd be too territorial. They already fight for favouritism amongst themselves.'

Your stomach churned for something sweet, so you turned around to walk back.

'Perhaps,' you thought as you walked home, 'it's just meant to be me and the snakes for all time.'

SNAKES

Written at home in Whitechapel

THE 47A GETS INTO THE DART station in the centre of town in about fifteen minutes. Good thing too, because I'm having to play host to these two bloody snakes racing each other inside my head. They make it completely impossible to focus on anything else. They're very evenly matched. If ever I close my eyes and stare at them long enough, I can barely determine a difference in their progress, and they keep exchanging the slight lead. They're slithering away as fast as they can, in perfect unison, parallel, like they were bitten by *my* eyes and have to make their escape.

As the bus pulls away from a stop or a light, my plastic poncho rustles really loudly on the seat. But I have to wear it for going into the pet shop, in case I come home smelling of a rabbit hutch. Mother's sense of smell has sharpened with age. I should ask about a goat while I'm there – can you get goats at a pet shop? Maybe outside town in one of them big warehouse ones …

The strange thing is, though, that once or twice I've caught them resting, the snakes – after being sure they could only flee – out of the corner of my eye. It's like they only race when they're absolutely sure I'm looking at them. Or they're keeping up pretences! To me? For what reason? Don't ask me.

Like they need an audience, or something to run away from? Why else would they behave different when being observed?

From the car park of the DART station, it's a four-minute walk to the pet shop across the river. I've it timed.

When the bus is moving and the snakes are resting, having their little pit stop, they sit coiled quietly beside each other, sipping milk from the same bowl. They prefer when I drink the goat's. And I prefer *them* when they're that way, relaxed. But heaven forbid I accidentally close my eyes and dwell a micro-second on them – and they sense it and take off running. Well, slithering. Fast.

Maybe they're scared of me, but they don't have to be. They're snakes – they've nothing I could want. Neither I nor they can benefit from perpetually fleeing their whole lives.

They're made from sort of elastic-band-type-looking material, it seems, from what I can see because they're always wriggling so quick. Dashing away into the undergrowth. I can barely get a decent glimpse to make a full inspection.

And they sing a definite something. I don't know why, I'd guess the same reason we do it: to keep spirits up. I see their little forky tongues flicking out in unison but I can't hear them, I can only see them. I tried to imagine their songs, but only in my rubbish imagination. I wondered if they convert war and brutality into songs like we do. No, of course they don't, Olly; they don't have those impulses. That's a narrow, human projection onto the minds of two pure, unsullied, innocent little creatures.

Then again, they're behind *my* lower eyelids, so maybe they share a few aspects of human weakness. They're clearly not very brave.

Not that it'd be easy to tell, but I have no choice but keep them secret, because Mother rules the roost and says no pets. As a proud native of this island since civilisations back, she's been privy to all the Old Magic but she refuses to share – well, not with me anyway. So her lips have formed deep crinkles around their edges. They look like they've been sewn shut. They might as well have been.

I sometimes sit cross-legged in the junction of the street outside our house in the evening. I'm never up hugely long before. East-south-east is the ideal direction to sit most of the time. To give the snakes a rest from all that rushing. Facing town and the headland, toward the sea.

Mother haunts me from the bedroom window and keeps a list of all the neighbours' comments and complaints.

*

It's funny how we were the exact same in many ways, me and Sal. Same face, same voice, same genes, almost the same smile. But opposite. Because I hate the sea, and I love the sand. On the beach next to the Cross of old Ceann Bhré, where we used be sent for Good Friday repentance. Peering down, keeping an eye on the whole strand and the direction everyone's going in, the pencilly auld nun of a witch.

I'd be shouting over the crashing waves as we put the towels down, 'It's whole civilisations, Sal, crumbled between our toes! All the people who already had their turn.'

Then Sal's eyes would go sideways, and she'd sideways jog to the sea. She always had this way of being rude but in a way where people responded to it. Gave her more for it. I was the opposite. 'Prrrtty much,' were the words she said.

Maybe I could present the snakes with the option to calm down, and have a discussion about why they're always in flight. I wouldn't be able to give them courage but I might be able to make them less scared. So that they stay in repose, quietly camped, lapping away with their two little tongue forks, instead of no time of mine being taken to send them fleeing into the dark. The cheek. They never get anywhere though; they never make a dent.

But if I could gift them with the ability to stop – 'Yeah. Just relax. Go on. You never get anywhere anyway, snakes. You never get away. But maybe that's not what you need.' I wish I knew what their needs were so I could go back to dealing with my own.

Maybe they're only comfortable when they're on the move.

If I made eye contact with a real snake, a big python that I saw down in the pet shop, say, maybe it would be able to spot two of its own inside and offer them some insight on how to be still. Like an outside snake. In repose, in the whole compass circumference, not just east-south-east.

I should try that, and if it doesn't work, I'll tell the pet-shop expert that I have two pet snakes and describe their habits and see what he suggests.

It couldn't hurt if the snakes became aware of a goat on the outside. Aware of us cohabiting peacefully, and of me drinking its milk regularly. But where would I keep it? If they don't notice, it's because they're too preoccupied focusing on all the bad things they've witnessed me do to give me any credit for a goat.

Like the night we stole Mother's alcohol. A dry Spanish sherry. We were only fourteen. Sal started and then I sucked up the rest. Mother had spilled it all over the glass coffee table and passed out after another night spent on the rosary beads. Going around and around them like a broken record. Quiet as it was possible to be, which was not very, we sucked it all up and I licked the table afterwards, a table I was aware hadn't been cleaned in weeks because it was my job to clean it.

Or the night walking back along Quinsborough Road, and I hit her a slap in front of all the nice houses, but I want to tell them, 'Snakes, I was only young and Sal told me John Lennon did it, and anyway she said things that were far worse than hitting. But hitting leaves a mark you can see, d'you see? Not like the Old Magic that puts marks on you in places you didn't even know were there.'

Maybe they were there fleeing us when we were born? Mother said I made such a fuss. I came out with the umbilical cord wrapped around my leg, and the wrap around my leg was causing the wrap around Sal's neck to choke her to death, and to all present I'm sure it wasn't unfunny. Like I fell out of the womb hellbent on dousing both of our candles that had only been lit for a grand total of seconds.

I feel like shouting at them, 'We're here and we can't share a body and constantly avoid each other!'

Why be always fleeing? Like in the Presentation Sisters. Like there was something wrong with me. They didn't know me enough. They only knew me by my worst quality, which Sal told me was inconsistency. I was a round lemon pip who couldn't make up its mind whether to plummet or float. Other folks didn't know what to do with that, she said. They found it unnerving.

It's not me, it's you, snakes. I mean it as a friendly reminder of the simple fact that we all have to share space, and for that you make me miserable? The only way you might ever stop running is if you get where you're going, but then where will you be? And what would be behind you then? What kind of destination would keep you slithering even though it knows you've already arrived? Limbo!

Jesus. Mother went through an even quieter phase after they took that out of the catechism. And a fat lot of good that did, as if people can suddenly turn around and say they don't believe in it. Limbo exists, that's the end of it. There's no uncasting that spell. That's probably where you're stuck, you poor wrigglers. Perpetually in flight.

I hope it's not raining there, or maybe you like the rain, I don't know. Maybe you're the opposite.

You see, this is the downfall of modern living. Because you can't have a thought without the risk of sabotaging it with a trillion more that are all being had in the same minute that all scream at you in unison parallel!

My god-given instinct is to try and show you that you're fleeing in the wrong direction. Limbo lies between heaven and hell and you're dashing into the dark ... which doesn't exactly spell heaven to me. But Olly. What do you know? Of course, I don't know, I don't have any knowledge on the subject. Maybe heaven's unlike the pictures, maybe heaven is actually in the absence of light. It's all guesswork until I consult the snake professional down at the pet shop.

The bus pulls in to do its loop-de-loop before continuing on towards Ballybrack.

I hope it's the tall bald fellow with the nice smile today. In the pet shop. He smirks without opening his mouth. He wears a salmon colour jersey often. Sorry, snakes, that *I* don't get to be your saviour. I've to settle for playing host.

When I walk in, how will I find the words to broach the question? Ahem, hello, excuse me, have you ever been present with a snake on its deathbed? When you were gathered around, did you get the impression that it was tending toward the darkness or the light in its final moments? Did it wriggle a certain way in the tank? Did you take it out of the tank because you knew it was dying, or because it was already dead?

Can snakes love, or are they just governed by instinctual impulses? How can I be sure that the snakes inside don't differ in other ways when compared to their traditional external brothers? No, that's a pointless question. I already know the answer to that.

The bus leaves me off in the DART car park. Even from here, you can't help hear the crashing of the shore. But thank god it's fairly still, so this poncho isn't glued to me.

I go down the street going past the pet shop, but it's closed. Tuesdays they close at 5 p.m., it says on the door. Then the tall salmon-polo-shirt fellow definitely isn't in …

I carry on walking through town. Someone's playing a piano badly out of a first-floor window, and burning some sweet wood. I imagine the list coiling around Mother's feet at home if that kind of racket was dinning through our junction.

There's a likeness of the snakes spray-painted in bright rainforest colours on a graffiti wall in Father Houlihan Terrace, across the junction from the vet hospital. They're being held in the arms of two smiling girls, one white, one black. Both with too many teeth. Even after the sunny day, the wall's always damp to the touch. The town is dead. Just the passing of the odd car. It must be gone seven o'clock in the evening – on what day, I couldn't guess. Oh, Tuesday.

It's not long before I need to relieve myself, so I drift over to the beachfront promenade toilets.

And down the strand, rubbing my eyes, walking right along the edge where the wet ends and the dry begins, facing myself off to the east-south-east direction. To give the snakes the best chance of a rest. Down beyond the headland, the lighthouse lantern revolving catches the skinny arm of auld Ceann Bhré.

The deafening crashing of them waves always upset me, ever since we were small. Since we first came down here. The way they leap up on the shore. Like the sea was angry with me. Sal was always the opposite.

I squeeze my toes around whole civilisations! Crumbled to sand! I didn't much care about living out our whole life, Sal. And the truth is … I come down here week after week after week and ask myself as sincerely as I can. Am I sorry? And still, the answer's no. It's strange. I expected it to have been opposite by now.

I've always *hated* the sea. But not as much as that Old, Dark Magic I felt when I was with you. When you were around.

And I genuinely thought you were waving at me. I one hundred per cent thought that, at least until the first instance of you going down. I remember it clearly, how the thought struck me, just a couple of moments later – how there's two of us. And one less isn't all that bad. Not on the scale of entire civilisations under our feet. All the ones who already had their turn.

Your eyes looked sideways. 'Prrrtty much' were the words you said. And then you ran off to have a swim.

Sideways jogging into the sea.

FRAYED

Written in Bristol

MAN SHUFFLE OFF an empty train carriage, that just pulled into (subterranean) subway station.

Grime-slicked tiles. Stinking payphone dark-green tone. Under the flickering fluorescent ceiling strip.

Man, and he burping a lot, like he got a lotta gas coming out of him. *Burp.* It's like green Pompeii. But, man, he shred them out slowly enough so they hiss through his six rotten green-tone teeth.

Man try to clear out what's lurking in the shadows at the back of his throat. *Ach! Ach!* He can't rightly remember what he ate …

Man, and he pulling up his old coat now to protect from the real fast tunnel chill. Man shuffle, blind as a subterranean tunnel mouse.

Blowing back from the steps leading up to the turnstile, other than the fleeing footsteps, is the blaring

BLAH BLAH BUBBLE BRRRRNNN of a trumpet horn, stuck to another man's face. A busker, let's call him Paul, who once was terribly bullied and had to have the power cord of a teakettle removed from his nine-year-old umbilicus canal due to blubbering over slitting his finger on some fish skin. That was when he was nine.

Man rest back on his worn heels for a sec to try to remember joy. When that don't work, he give a hock, spit and a jump! And under his hood does a great big jaw unlock and heaves in a Big Gulp of breath. Then he creepy-crawls along the seating stalls to close the gap between Man and this busking trumpet morsel.

Paul is all swagger and sway, from the knees beneath his tight ripped jeans, to try to shake a feeling to the surface he felt way back when he can't rightly remember … benign beginnings and the capable playing of his trumpet. Paul likes doooom jazz. He makes a healthy living on top of a living this way, does Paul. The money he mostly saves.

Man clasp his dirty hands with the too-long fingernails. 'Oh, please?' Man plead, as Paul sways. 'Ooh, please, play "Home on the Range"?'

Man, and he squealing now over trumpet Paul, who plays 'Careless Whisper' in a careful whispering tone to be clever, but it's getting spoilt.

Man spit through his teeth. 'Play.'

Man unlock his jaw to open his mouth as wide as it can go. 'Ooh, please, PLEASE play "Home on the Range"? My favourite! My mommy NEVER STOP singing that song, fuck. I see the old range for miles.

Outside my window. Where the bunnies hop but there was no nothing but concrete block. Giant slabs of nothing held together by rot! Haa, kiddy. I miss they bunny company they good company, you know?'

Man clutching hold of himself now and lurching over bent double. Man, and he just won't stop stomping and pleading and making a circle like he calling up the recent dead, with the music and lyrics coiling around his head.

'Where seldom is HEARD [stomp], a something stink word [bow]. A skunk and a piece of a play?'

Man, but he won't leave Paul alone. With the cooing and the whining and the begging in that miserable tone.

'Where seldom is heard [kick]. An unsavoury word now [lurch]. No?'

Under the flickering fluorescent ceiling strip, *Brrrrn* goes Paul's trumpet. I ain't ever gonna dance again – you got that right, Paul. Filthy feet ain't *got* no reason.

Paul stops playing 'Careless Whisper' and the silence rings out in chains. It nearly kills them both. A bill that begs for a steel blast of train. But now, there ain't no trains. It's late. It's so late all the trains decided to stop or bypass our station to avoid Man and give Man some respite to do what needs to get done.

'Oh, yes, please? Oh, why won't you, please? For little old me? I don't have nobody.'

Paul makes no Man eye contact, because all eye contact is bad. Only escalate the thing further. Paul bends down to close his trumpet case full of coins, and some few notes. He hasn't done so bad. Maybe just enough for a full hot salted beef with a side on the side in Katz's.

Man try to punch a hole in the ceiling as he turn out his tracksuit pockets. 'Yes! Yes! You see I got no money.'

But Paul forgot to put his trumpet in his case before he closed his case, and now he feels like an idiot. He closed his case too fast before scraping out all the coins to avoid scratching the brass of his horn or the horn of his brass.

Man grin, staring into space. 'You can see, I hear you closed your case and you ready to take me Home is what I want. That what will make my century, yes?'

Paul's clutching his trumpet in his hand distracted, trying to struggle free of George's lyric about feet. He's trying to resign himself to the fact that that's not it, the lyric. That it's something else.

Man stop stomping. He go completely still. He splay out his arms out like Christ. Jesus Christ. Or one of the thieving animals who got mounted just behind him to boost the points of his Holy.

Man very slooowly raise his dirty hands. Ready for the nails of the notes to pierce through so he can drink his own blood.

His grimy green coat spreads out like wings that, if they hadn't been exposed to the big oil scandal, they could've blasted him off with such lift that he'd smash a hole right through the ceiling.

Man collapse to his knees and pray. 'Ooh, f-f-f-fuck, please?'

Paul can see the red horizontal lines of his fingers through the filth. Man void a deep grassy-green burp out in a hiss. Spittle of a non-human colour gathers in the corners of Man mouth. Head bowed down and with no one around.

Paul blushes, he glances up and down. Looking for eye contact to reference a frown. But there's nobody. They've all been delivered by the train. Down the mouth of the tunnel.

Man shuffle his knees a little bit closer to Paul's. 'Oh, yes. Now! Please.'

Man pupils dilate, as he begs prostrate. 'Please take me, home on the range, please? Take me home, take me. Home. Take me. Take me. Take me, please?'

Paul swallows, then looks right to give his left-brain sight.

Man cheer. 'Yes! Yessss. Yes. Goody.' Man salivating onto his chin now, because in the light of Paul's memory, he can see the "Home on the Range" song. Flickering in some old movie, black and white with a cowboy guy with smiling eyes all smug, lit in a ray of soft circle light. And somehow Man don't know, but in the old VHS tape memory, the cowboy guy's stalk of wheat stays sitting in his mouth, even as he smiles and laughs and flirts with a cowgirl with a lasso on her shoulder and wearing a patterned shirt like a tablecloth. The old lazy fiddle leads the cowboy in, wanting him to go (harmoniously so) into the first notes of surrender that gather on Paul's lips, as he lifts the horn and foolishly submits –

Home *Brrrrn* on the Range,
Where the *Brrrrn* and the *Brr-rrn* play,
Where *Brr*-dom is heard
A discouraging *Brrr*
And the skies are not bloody all –

Man eat him up.

Man unlock his jaw to make his mouth as wide as it can go, and gobble up Paul in one. No chew. Big. Gulp. *Burp!* Paul gas …

But, man, that silence how it rings out in chains. It's a bill that begs for a steel blast of train. Until Man hock – *ach, ACH!* – up a stubborn something that he can't rightly remember, that's lurking beyond the shadow at the back of his throat, *ach!* Furball? *Ach!* Until it coughs itself up and clangs on the ground.

Man, but he get low quick and sniff sniff at the horn.

Surrender on it sweet, but is brass fit to eat? Under the flickering fluorescent ceiling strip. Sniff sniff, anyway. Way to chew? No, no surrender, no consume. It only submitted to former Paul. And Man got no way to make it *Brrrr*, to drown out the last of his muffled cries coming from inside.

Man punch himself in the coat. 'Shhh.'

Man gather up the horn and snuggle it somewhere under his greasy armpit. He shuffle slowly away toward the steps up to the turnstile, singing in a careless tone,

Home, home on the RANGE,
Where the deer and the antelope play,

Where seldom is heard,
A discouraging word [lurch],
And the skies something bloody all daaaay ['Help!'].

'Shhh!'
Burp.

DESERT DONKEY LEGS

Written on a plane to Dubai

FUCKING HAMSTRINGS ARE MY FAVOURITE. Uh, they're such a treat. No matter how much I stretch them, no matter how much I push them past the point of protest to a warm, OK, kind of human place, the very next morning I wake up and they're as stiff as ever. They're such a pain in the ass, well, lower ass, and I read they can often be the cause of back pain too, so they're not content in being a localised annoyance, they also have to try to persuade other bits of you to join their cause in helping to ruin your day.

My job makes them much worse too because if I'm not sitting sedentary in a meeting, I'm sitting sedentary on the airplane with nowhere to stretch without risking involuntary flatulence, looking like a half-drunk fool or getting in the way of the flight attendants.

I'm forever stretching out on sandy-beige hotel carpets. It wouldn't do to carry on like that in the airport lounge. Once, before our morning meeting in the Minneapolis office, I went to a sports therapist – I never went back. This lady's eyes went wide when she said, 'You *have* to stretch more.' And she patted me in a kind of pitying way. Music to my ears …

Best hope is to balance out the drinks input and pray for sleep.

Then one night late on the red-eye, he came to me in a vision.

Where I'm standing sedentary, in the rolling dunes of a vast, hot desert. With nowhere to go. The sky is a dangerous blue. The sun has burnt up the clouds. Through the shimmer of the heat and the squint of my sweating brow, I see this figure who's standing stock still, somehow cast in shadow in the height of the killing sun.

I try to call out to him but no sound leaves my mouth. He shimmers far away like a mirage but it feels like he's probably there. I suddenly become afeared that this figure has no good intentions for me. I think about running – to where, I don't know – but opt to stay put for a change, because I'm rapidly weakening in the scorching heat and he stands full-postured like a boxer. Like the heat isn't bothering him in the slightest, so I conclude that if he wants to run me down, he could.

Then he moves! And keeps moving. He is sprinting towards me across the dunes. Panting, stood still, I decide I'm best off turning down the volume on the voice encouraging me to shit myself inside the robes of my Bedouin garb – a fat lot of good that would do.

Then he's fifty yards away and his strides burst into bows of leaps and bounds. His gait makes no sense to me. He earns himself height in the jump but the sand makes his impact quiet.

Now he is ten yards away, and when the shimmer finally subsides, I drop my cupped hands and loosen my cramping facial muscles to absorb what's in front of me. He's Me.

A calm, steely-eyed Me. Me that's definitely me, but isn't.

Me is showing me Me by catching my gaze, but there's no challenge in it. More of a kindly request. The sand flaps his hair up and down and the wind swirls the sand behind him until it takes on the form of a field of corn.

It feels pleasant to listen to the absence of my panic.

Truer Me. An impression that somehow bears more resemblance to me than me. I take him in. He is naked. He is a grizzled, more weather-worn Me but in a rugged, piratical way. He doesn't have to squint in the glaring sun. He doesn't have to pant after his huge bounding run. The space in me absorbs him piece by piece, downward, from his dark-pools-with-flecks-of-yellow eyes. And everything seems to be the same down to the mole orbiting his right nipple, until we get to the legs.

His are the legs of a beast. I stare at them for a long time, trying to remember if that's what my legs really look like in the mirror.

A hint of challenge twinkles in his dark pools.

With my gaze fixed on his beast legs, I do a slow flick-through of the beast-of-burden rolodex in my head.

Goat (maybe I shouldn't have flicked straight to goat because a quick pang of worry hums that I've offended him – he might think that I thought he was some sort of devilish satyr) ... sheep ... Jersey bull ... bison ... water buffalo ... llama? I am keeping horse for last or nearing last because, somewhere deep down, I know it is that or something like that. Definitely not camel.

Horse ...? His gaze intensifies but doesn't change.

Donkey? The fonts of water in his eyes overflow and pour into me through mine, and a knowing glow passes across his face and across my poor heart, or maybe it's my stomach.

I look down, and *my* legs are now donkey legs.

I raise up a hoof and hold it in the far hand. I trim out the bits of old clogged sand. I do the same with the other. They feel like standing on two jet-propelled pogo sticks.

I stamp them in the sand, and underneath I feel all the animals that have buried themselves for the day to avoid the killing sun wake up from the vibration of my powerful hooves and hindquarters and squirm a bit to tell me that they're annoyed at the early alarm clock and please keep it down so they can continue to sleep.

After all, they have a concert to perform later, gathering food for themselves and all of their progeny and future descendants. Every moment of an animal's life is vital to the survival of their species so they deserve an undisturbed rest. This thought is followed by a wave of gratitude for the fact that a part of my body is now the body of an animal. Hopefully, it means that every part of *my* life garners some importance to the survival of my species – donkey-legged human people.

I look back to my new friend and he's now me from before, from the waist down anyway. His legs are now my previous legs. Me has given of his legs and taken my old, tight human legs.

My ex-legs make no pain peep because they aren't there any more! Woohoo!

I ask him without breath or words, *Will you be OK out here in this hostile desert environment? Searching for food and fleeing from predators without your magic donkey legs?*

But his insides just laugh and give my poor heart a rest.

I swivel my big strong hooves to savour them. Savour the glory of them – but quietly, mind, so as not to rouse the rest of the poor moles and mice and scorpions and snakes and camel spiders who have a whole concerto to perform later.

I backheel the sand away and stretch my new legs out in a lunge, in another lunge, and then off I go running. Sprinting. Full tilt. Full blast. Tooth and nail! God up in heaven playing a digital harp on a cloud, do they feel good. They're bounding like I'm on pure air. Every hoof hit can feel the Earth tremor in fear and respect beneath me.

A wail of primal joy comes from somewhere down in my pelvis. From where man's spirit lives, where he projects his physical form.

The sand flies in my eyes and I can't stop screaming. I'm sprinting so fast I have to stomp down a small twinge of worry that I'm going to end up so far out into the desert that I'll be lost, really lost, but then I remind myself that I'm already lost! And keep running.

After miles and miles and miles and God knows how many miles, I slow down slowly to a light trot and then to a reluctant halt. The red shadows are stretching and the moon is gathering company in an explosive sky. My legs are tired and throbbing, and I've worked up a note of thirst – excuse me, flight attendant?

I'm not too worried, though. This desert may look barren, but the ringing of a little bell inside lets me know it has everything I could possibly need in abundance.

My tired legs turn me round to my right and I find a bit of crag. I scrap around in the hardened sand under the rocks until the spring reveals itself to the surface. I yield to the caution that scans around in all directions to make sure I'm alone – and not because I've seen animals like me do it in nature documentaries and I am copying their cautious behaviour, no. It comes out of a million years of hardwired instinct that obviously comes as a bonus with the legs.

When the sandy coast is confirmed clear, I dip my head down low to take a refreshing drink. It is magnificent.

The cool, healing water babbles above the sand and over my tongue, all flopped out. My tongue stays flopped out and lapping for a long time, *blaaaaasss.* Until I'm truly lost under the artesian sensation.

I take a knee and lay down. I press my face against the starlit Earth. Beneath her sandy make-up, I can hear her heartbeat.

I can hear every animal gurgling and grumbling in the corridor kingdom of the ground. Warming up their instruments for the concerto, as the sun whispers good luck with a thumbs up before she settles fully down. I can feel my own life-force drumming on the hoof, drumming along in sync. I am to be the main percussion of the Desert Orchestra. I will keep all the animals moving in time.

I kick away the sodden sand. I backheel it until the patch is fully dry. Then I take a nice long, deep breath, all the way down to the food junction where animal meets the divine, then I launch from my haunches into a mighty leap, as far up to the stars as I can go, and land in a mighty sonic *BOOM* to announce to the other players that I'm ready to play. I have never been more ready to play. Let the concerto *commence*!

Then I'm awoken in the airplane seat and my chin is spittled and there's blood coming from somewhere. I've spilled whiskey and coke all over myself. The attendant, in a red waistcoat and hat, is fiercely shaking me by the shoulder, next to another one with a nose full of red napkins.

The lady directly opposite me in the business pantsuit is picking her newspaper off the aisle floor and giving me daggers.

I hope I haven't farted ... I wipe off my spittle and rear myself up in the seat to do a quick panic-scan of all the other faces in my vicinity. Some are frowning, some aren't even bothering to avoid my eye. Some are red in the face from laughter and avoiding my eye any way they can – behind a bobbing newspaper or by turning their head to look over their shoulder at a bare wall of nothing. I've cracked the little screen in front but the flight attendants haven't clocked it yet.

I catch sight of the lit-up green man at the top of the aisle and leap to my feet to make a beeline for the toilets, but my legs are asleep and they crumple me straight back down in the aisle, like a pathetic sack of shit. Everybody's feet flinch. My feet are gone, my hamstrings are as tight as a drum and I cannot straighten my legs.

A disjunct chorus of sniggers, snorts and squeaks erupts as my face comes to rest on the floor, all littered with spilled crisps and damp with wine. The shards and the crumbs dig into my cheekbone. For a moment, I shut my eyes and go limp, and try to tune out the barking attendants. 'Sir, you have to get up off ...'

And for the microest of micro time, down in the hum of the jet, I can hear it. Just below. Just out of my reach.

The abundant desert. All the little sleepy ants and owls and golden moles and snakes and chameleons and meerkats and mice and scorpions and larks and sandy cats and crocodiles and foxes and lizards and camel spiders are yawning and stretching and coming out of their caves. I try to tap my hoof because my big drum-solo is coming up on the beat. And squeak and snuffle and burrow and snort and four, three, two, one …

But the powerful pins and needles drag me back aboard and remind me that I don't have hooves. They crash like cymbals in my toes and up my legs. I bite my lip and fight the needles hard. With a grip of the arm rests, I drag myself along the aisle like a newborn foal. I manage as far as the curtain, but by the time I have it pulled, the little green man has turned red!

So I prop myself against the part with all the drawers and bits to wait.

My left leg is still kicking out the needles and I can't get it to stop. If I do stop, the numbness will return. A spot of turbulence gets us, which shunts me and the two flight attendants into a stand-off over the fact that the seatbelt light is now on. I put my hand up to pacify, as if to say, *Please, please – I'll be as quick as I can.*

But it has the wrong effect, and the bloody-nosed one does a flinch.

The toilet finally comes free. I put the lid down and lock the door and drop my head into my hands and sigh. Sitting for a while to soothe my poor heart, while I wait for the pins and needles to disappear, so that my legs can go back to being fully dead.

TREASURE

Written in Bali

I'VE BEEN DRIVING A VAN for seventeen year. She's not the worst, but it sticks in my craw that I don't own her. She's been my beast of burden for seventeen long years, longer than all of my relationships, and frankly way less demanding.

When she works well, and mostly she does, we're in a state of great symbiosis, but it's company policy that they never sell their vans to staff. Permanent loan is the best I can do. That's their first mistake. They tried to replace her a few times, but every time I've told them if you lose the van, you lose me. They knew I was serious when I offered to pay for the necessary repairs out of my own wages.

They called me loyal and stubborn – exactly what they're looking for in their employees, so they kept us on. Beats working in an office. And no one knows her like I do. She needs a very specific hand and that hand is mine. There are few things in this world I'm exceptional at but one of them is making her run like an absolute gem.

I work with another fellow, John Buggy. The Buggyman, we call him. He rides passenger. We don't speak much. Correction. *He* doesn't speak much. He's a little tyke, but I'd say he'd fair go through you for a shortcut. Always doing press-ups when he thinks I'm not looking. But no craic in the van. I'm just talking away to myself for nine hours. Like sucking blood from a stone. And always trying to get his oily fingers on her steering wheel. I have to take her keys and lock the van when going into a shop, so he's not sitting in the driver side when I come out.

Now, the company's second mistake is allowing their drivers to take their vans home of an evening, 'cos that's when I get the full benefit out of her. After a long day, there's nothing I like more than to go on a treasure hunt. It's how I blow off steam.

I looked it up recently. The definition of treasure is something that has perceived collective value and is usually hidden or kept in a safe place. And that's usually because it's rare, or rare and shiny, depending on how clever the civilisation is. But not always. Something can have collective value and not be rare or shiny – often the opposite. And that's the kind of treasure me and my girl go hunting of an evening for. In fact, it's everywhere if you know where to look, and the more 'shiny' it is, let's say, the less I'd be into catching it 'cos who wants to draw that kind of attention to themselves?

Everybody has a passion, and this is mine. Some people might object, but fuck 'em. The world is a cruel and indifferent place.

What I do is, I sit and wait outside the local function hall. The town isn't massive so you can usually predict where crowds of them are going to be and what nights. I keep a pair of them compact binoculars in the glovebox, to watch them flood out after a dance lesson or an art lesson or gymnastics – personal favourite – all screeching and giggling, eyes all wide with adrenaline and excitement. All giddy from seeing each other outside the walls of the school. No uniforms. They dress to impress. All pink in the face from doing handstands, jumping up and down and squeaking in their shorts or leggings. It'd make any man's drawers quiver. Then their little heads start snapping from side to side, searching around for their parents. I love that look when you catch it through the compacts. It's always the same. First, the eyebrows are all furrowed, looking around for Mammy and Daddy. Then if there's no Mammy and Daddy, their faces go a kind of strange blank, and they drift up and down the path. They go into themselves a small bit. This is a great sign. When that happens, I can hear myself salivating. Every time. Because that's them considering doing something adventurous. Like setting out to make it home by themselves. And when you zoom in on them on the compacts, it's mad: it's like the two of you are face to face.

But most of them file away into cars – that part can take a fucking age. The sifting stage. That's by far the most time-consuming stage of the evening. Shaking the panhandle. Hopping into cars they are, saying good-byes and texting, taking all day. Then you see the one who didn't have a lift lined up. Or Daddy forgot. Or his parents decided he was old enough to walk home. That's when the real treasure hunt begins. The lone ones are usually staying on to juice the last of the social scene, but not always – sometimes they file away off to be alone with their thoughts. Them ones I'm less inter-ested in. I like the ones that love to be around people, the ones that are working hard to impress you. They're easier to catch and more exciting to hold onto because they're the ones who genuinely believe that it'd be a terrible, terrible tragedy if something were to happen to them.

The introverted ones are more muted. Less bright-ness in the eyes. They sort of disappear into themselves. They go all blank and pensive and that just lifts the lead right out of my pencil, if I'm honest. I can usually spot those ones early on if I've picked one up, and I can quickly send them on their way after giving them enough encouragement never to speak about our little meeting to anyone. You just pull the van over, get up right close, and get a good strong hauld of them by the scruff. You lock in with their eyes, and you tell them, 'Now, say nothing.' It's important to hold eye contact with them for at least four or five seconds, else the warning won't work.

But the other ones, they're a treasure. They're the Forty Thieves' cave and I'm Ali Baba, but instead of taking one bag I'm taking the whole fucking lot!

So tonight, I'm sat quiet in the van. You never know how long these fuckin' gymnastics classes are going to go on for … Buzz down the window and spark a fag. I've put my nice long going-out coat on, to hide the oily overalls. And my darling is fizzing away in that comforting way under the dashboard. That lovely fizzing you hear when you've just turned her off. Like a prize colt panting after winning the Grand National. Oh, we do make a good team.

The auld fella's passed away now about what, ten year? I think on him sometimes, wonder where he is. I hoped Mammy would soon follow but to everyone's surprise she held on for dear life, for the best part of another decade. Doing it to spite me, the auld bitch. He used to love to come clattering into my room all hours of the night. Drunk, of course. She wouldn't move a muscle next door, pretending she was asleep. Then she'd lay in bed all the next day. Quiet as a mute. Pretending to be sick. But if it was a Sunday, sure, me and him would get the big fry on ourselves and then head off to a match.

When she did finally die, I ignored her final wishes and had her cremated instead. I had other plans. She wanted to be put in a box to try and put off rotting for as long as she could. If you ask me, that's the most barbaric of all the customs, the Christian one. Like you're hoping you'll come back too. Such vanity involved in it. My take is when you're gone, you're gone, and that's it. It doesn't matter what happens to your remains. You never owned it in the first place, you were just borrowing it, so why should you be bothered about what happens to it after you shuffle off this mortal coil? It's like moving out of a flat you rented for years and then coming back every week, nosing in on the renovations. Anyways, I burned her.

I gave her the cremation. Right around the time my darling needed a new paint job, and I told work that I'd do it. They love my dedication to their property. I mixed my mother's ashes up into the paint and I daubed her all over my van. There she still sits, the two ladies in my life bound together for eternity. Although she'd probably disapprove of the hunt. I hope she's not having to witness what's going on around her remains, else she'll have a few things to say to me when I join her in heaven, I can tell you that.

Time to catch a fish. A little black-tracksuited chap's just skipped round the corner of the darkened side of the hall, onto Sapphire Lane. Christ, the parents of this one are asking for it! Sapphire Lane's perfect. The houses don't start till you go up the road around the corner. Before that, it's all boarded-up shops and empty units above.

I cruise up. 'Give us a backflip!'

Little treasure stops and a look of shock comes across his face, the likes of which would make any man's drawers quiver.

'What?'

'You were in doing gymnastics tonight. My little fella was too, but he got a lift home from his friend's mam instead, so here I am like a thick with no one to drop home. Do a backflip and I'll give you a lift. Go on.'

The little fella stands frozen, all sheepish under the orange streetlamp, in a black tracksuit and runners with graphics on them.

He pouts. 'I can't do a backflip yet. But I can do a handstand.'

He takes off his bag and drops it on the ground and centres his stance. Oho, lads, we have one on the line. He's taking it so seriously. I try and slow my breath 'cos I can hear the saliva jets and for a minute I think he'll hear them too. What an eejit. He is wiping at the ground with his sleeve.

'Careful now, good man!' I say. 'I don't want to be taking you home with gravel in your hands!' Said with a stroke of sincerity too because I do not want gravel in his hands, for obvious reasons.

He does a few rounds of trying. Pitiful. But I give him a few claps and a 'Wahey' and a big encouraging thumbs up and then, moment of truth, I lean over and open her passenger door. She creaks as the door swings open – fuck! I must remember to top her up with a bit of motor oil.

Suddenly a bizarre thought – that creaking's Mammy, trying to stop me, and the door doesn't actually need any oil at all – but I force that meddling bitch out of my head best I can and force a big smile onto my face.

I'm always a bit reluctant to smile at them, though, on account of the fact that I'm missing a front tooth and it puts them off. Because of the rugby, I never bothered to get them fixed. Sure, what for?

It's spooked the little lad a small bit, I can see, so I close my mouth, concealing my ugly gaps when I say, 'Hop in there, Spider-Man. I'll drop you home and you can thank my young fella in the morning for having such a generous auld fella.'

Always plant the seed that you're a dad, always. Works every time.

The little lad looks up the dark of Sapphire Lane, then down the road towards the town. A look of slight weariness comes across his face. 'OK.'

He scrapes his feet all the way over to my cab and hops in. He struggles so adorably on the steps! I am not counting my chickens, but he might be the finest in my collection, if I can get him home. Stay calm for our guest, my darling, no fuck-ups now.

We start driving up the road. Weirdly, he doesn't even tell me where he lives. It's like he knows what's happening and has accepted it, which is fine by me. There are three stages of danger on the way back, and by danger, I mean areas with street lights and round-abouts. There are so many roundabouts in this fucking country. We're forever getting lost going around in circles. Fucking crowd running the place wouldn't know their arse from their elbow.

'Who's that on your runners, then? Spider-Man?'

'No, Mephisto.'

'Who?'

'Mephisto. He's not a superhero, he's a villain.'

'Devilish-looking lad. I like your style, kid!' Quick slap on the leg and give his knee a little pinch. Nothing. He stares out the window.

Through stage one, and back into darkness and comfort. My girl always performs better in the darkness.

Coming up on danger-zone two. There won't be that many people around 'cos it's Wednesday, and the town's a ghost town these days all week. But still, I'll breathe a sigh of relief once we're out the other side.

From out of her dashboard panel comes a strange little creaking sound. From somewhere under the hood … Which I choose to ignore 'cos I'm too busy engaging the kid in as much banter as I can to keep him distracted.

But the creaking is turning into a growling, scraping sound, and I see it register on the lad's face – how dare he, the little bastard. I'm absolutely mortified with embarrassment. Girl, do not let me down now, do not let me down. Not tonight of all nights, not after seventeen years of smooth sailing, not tonight.

We're beyond halfway through danger-zone two, it being the most dangerous, the crest of the mountain, if you will, 'cos it's the town centre.

'So, what does Mephisto do that's so spe–?'

BANG! An ear-curdling grinding noise is followed by a loud, rending *thump* and a big splash, and my beloved seizes up – she fucking seizes up. The steering wheel goes completely rigid. She's locked me out! Why would she do this to me now, the cunt! After all this time!

This can't be her. I was right in my intuition earlier, and wrong to ignore it. This *is* Mammy. She always suspected my ways but never had the courage to say anything while she was alive. Well, she's getting her own back now. Fuck, fuck, fuck. The van has stalled, right in the middle of town.

'Hold on there.'

I pop the hood and leap out like my arse is on fire. Opening her bonnet, I'm hit with a black billow of smoke. I've seen this before. I drop to my belly, don't give a fuck that I'm staining the front of my long coat, and what I see on her belly confirms the worst. That she's missing a big piece. The bastarding pan's after falling clean off the van. She's dropped all her oil and seized up the engine! That might be her wrote off now. Fuuuuuuck. Work are going to be furious, I forgot to change her oil. And since I'm the one volunteering to keep her in tip-top shape, they'll blame this on me.

I jump to my feet and spit 'Fuck it' through gritted teeth.

From behind me, 'Having a bit of trouble there?'

I know that voice. It's an accent from not round here. There's only two people that could be. The Protestant priest Father Okonkwo, or O'Casey the guard who was stationed up here from Cork. He shines a light on my face. My ugly, gap-toothed, disgusting face sitting atop a filthy, dirty oil- and sweat-stained coat.

His light darts from my face into the cab. I feel an intense flood of dread as he lands the light of his torch onto the face of my little treasure inside.

O'Casey's face falls. My knees fall. I have no run in me. In a way, I feel kind of relieved.

He slams me back face down onto the rat-level asphalt and jams his knee into my back with unnecessary force, while he spits through his own teeth. 'So it's *you*, ya cunt ya? You're the one's been doin' it.'

He slaps cuffs onto my wrists – big fucking ouch! – but I don't grimace. I feel kind of calm, actually. Strangely, it's the calmest I've felt in a while. I'm sure the panic will kick in later on when the whole town finds out. No big surprise, they'll say. Like father, like son.

Shame the auld fella didn't make it this far. I could've done with a familiar face inside. O'Casey drags me up and hauls me into the cruiser.

The Buggyman! Jesus wept. John the Buggyman will have his greasy mitts all over her now, that's if she doesn't get scrapped. Jesus Christ tonight. He won't make her run right. He won't give a shit about her. She needs a very specific hand and that hand is mine.

I watch O'Casey going over to get the kid out of my cab. Bit low energy, the lad. Moves like a little auld fella. Like he's made of paper mâché. No wonder he can't do a backflip. He wouldn't've been the finest in my collection.

Maybe I should've buried her after all … Mammy. Even in death, she can still really pick her moments.

Ha, funny. Betrayed, by the only two women I've ever made the mistake of loving. What a clown. I think that's what they call the tragicomedy genre, like when you're picking out a film to rent.

I should write this later on inside. Give me something to do. It could make a film. 'Two broke women
…' something. Something like that for the tagline. Sure,
someone might get a laugh out of it.

HOUSE IN THE COUNTRY

Written (mostly) in Toronto

ONE OF IAN'S IDIOT CRONIES taped over my *House in the Country*. Probably Twat. All my *H in the C* tapes are stacked up beside the TV, all thirty-two of them. Two hundred and sixty-six episodes. Plus Christmas specials. Clearly labelled: DO NOT TAPE OVER. ON PAIN OF DEATH. None of them will own up. Ian doesn't care. I told him about it. He told me I'm eleven now and that means I have to stop watching so much TV and I have to convert the TV into something cool for all his little groupies. Like a fish tank. He said he has faith in me that I will put it to some good use. That it would be easy.

IAN: Just make sure to plug the thing out first!

Bad things always come in threes. But Mum said that only meant big things. I can't tell if this is a big enough thing to count.

Whoever it was taped over it with some stupid old documentary where lots of people live together, like here, but in a sunny country – I don't know what one. And in tents. The documentary cuts in on the tape right as the opening credits to the first episode of *H in the C* end. The people all wear the same purply colour. They cry in a barn. And they hug each other. One of them eats that big fruit with a machete, where it looks like bashing someone's head open. They cry lots on the video. And there isn't piles and piles and piles of boxes of loads of stuff, like there is here. Boxes of magazines and coat hangers and clothes, and paint and oil tins stacked to the ceiling. And shit and insects and crap everywhere. They cry lots, on the video, but it's sunny there. It's never sunny here. I don't even know how many are living here any more. Sometimes you won't see one of them for weeks. You think that one must have left and gone back to his parents' house, then a week later he'll wake up somewhere in the mountains of crap and wander downstairs, sleepy and confused looking.

We can't skip the ads on our TV. It is very old. I had a friend six years ago, Jeremy Seal. His mum's TV could skip ads. I only went to his house once and she gave us warm rice pudding with two kinds of jam. He had a remote control that could turn on and off other TVs. I did not break it but we are not friends any more.

Sponsored by blah blah ... it finally comes on. The rerun of the first episode of *House in the Country* that got taped over. It has taken a year and six months. I can retape it to recomplete my collection. I am not missing it. It is a Special episode, where they do a House in Another Country. They are in Hawaii.

I feel a shit coming on. But there's no rush. Things have finally calmed down. I hope. It must. I did not wake up and have the runs this morning. The toilet upstairs is broken. I have been going in a ditch down the lane towards the road. I like to go back and see all the flies the next day.

Twat sits in the armchair next to the couch. He picks at the foam on the armrest. He flicks a cockroach off his baggy jeans. He sits like he's in a coma. He breathes through his mouth and texts with the click on. I can hear every click of every letter he types with his goat thumbs. *Ffffff, ffffffffffff, ffffffffffff.* I will watch this episode again later, in the middle of the night when even the bugs are asleep. Twat is here on purpose.

He doesn't like me watching *House in the Country*. He says it's because of Ian but it's actually because he doesn't like that I have all the knowledge to become a successful TV presenter like Jules Dixon when I'm older. He is jealous.

> TWAT: Ian says you're to have your bath before he gets home.

Where did this fool hear that I do baths? I want to stab Twat in the ribs with a compass that Ian's friend left here in that maths set. I would bury it in Twat but I'm afraid I would be doing him a favour by making him smarter. Or less ugly.

I fire a slipper at the TV. But I miss. It lands in a boat of old chips and ketchup. But Hooty doesn't care. He thinks he is the boss, but Ian is the boss. Twat thinks he's the next boss, but I am the next boss. Ian told me, just me. But Hooty does whatever he likes. His long antennae drift slowly around, back and forth. He is so distracting, and this is the episode where Jules is wearing clothes that people wear to the beach. The leaves of all the trees are big and fat and there are lots of little fountains. Note to self: include water feature in my future house in the country. Just one. Two maximum – I don't want to go overboard. Hooty sits on the TV screen because he knows that if I ever caught him, I would pull off his feelers and make him eat them. Stamp him into the carpet, but no, not to do that. Ian says the more you kill, the more show up. For the funeral. Ian says I only don't like them because they're German. Because I'm Grandad. He gives everybody nicknames. I call him lots of things back, but mostly Bloodshot.

Hooty is so annoying. He always sits right on the TV screen. Ian says be nice to Hooty. He says Hooty puts the TV to better use than me – as a tanning salon. I can tell it's him because he is the biggest one that lives by the TV. Twat says he heard him hiss once. But he's lying because I hissed at Hooty once for an hour but he didn't hiss back. Hooty likes me, but I do not like him. He sits right on Jules's mouth, every time it cuts back to Jules's face. Jules is so annoyed at Hooty too but he just won't move.

I hate Hooty and all of Hooty's children. And friends and parents and everyone in his whole world. Because he is everywhere. I have to pick them out of my bed before I go to sleep. I have to be careful touching anything anywhere, in case it moves. Specially in the kitchen and bathroom. The cockroaches are not the only ones. They have friends. Friends who fly and bite. Friends who build webs. Ian wanted to do his Ned Kelly thing last week. He told Twat to get a metal pot and a big spider inside bit him. Its web was really thick and white. Twat cried like a little twat. It was so funny.

One time I stomped three cockroaches at once. Ian walked into the kitchen and caught me.

ME: No, it's bubble wrap, it's bubble wrap!

He went red in the face, under the beard. He dragged me outside and Twat ran to find a rope. When I was tied, Twat pointed behind himself.

TWAT: Form an orderly queue!

They all wandered out of the house blinking into the sun. Seven or eight of them. None of them knew what they were queueing for. Twat kicked me with his big skater shoes. A lot of the boys had no shoes and their feet were black as muck. And so skinny – barely any of them could throw a proper kick.

EVERYONE ELSE: That's a big roach! Stomp him until all his juices go splat! STAMP HIM, STAMP HIM, STAMP HIM!

Ian did not stamp me. He just got his stupid little cronies to do it. After, when we were disinfecting my cuts, Ian pulled me close.

IAN: Nothing is rational. Rational doesn't exist. Real doesn't exist. But you know what exists? Love. I only raise a hand in love, little man. Only ever in love.

To where I could hear the breathing in his chest.

IAN: Those little critters in the kitchen are eating, drinking and breathing just like you and me. Nobody is god. Nobody is the devil. But I'm the boss!

Then he got me in a headlock. It hurt but it was meant to be fun so I laughed.

IAN: I'm the boss and you're my lieutenant. You hear? You're my right-hand man.

That's how I know I outrank Twat. I notice Twat's loud breathing and loud texting stop. *Ffffff*, stop.

TWAT: Hey, you.

I don't look at him, I just look at the TV.

TWAT: Which do you think sounds better? 'This is extremely serious and I appreciate you take it serious as well.' Or, 'This is extremely serious and I appreciate you take it extremely serious as well.'

I just look at the TV for ages. For the two of us to forget we were ever talking. But he won't move on. He won't breathe or click.

> ME: About what? What serious thing? Did you tape over one of my tapes?

Twat lets out a slow-moving snort. Like, how dare you, just tell me. I just ignore him. He just stares at me. Twat only ever looks at you out the corner of his eye, all evil, like a goat. Even if you're right in front of him. He has little rectangle goat pupils.

> ME: Neither. If it was you, I'll hurt you. In your sleep.

> JULES DIXON: Does this feel like the sort of place you two could call home?

> TWAT: You don't know where I sleep.

When Jules asks the guests a question, he makes it into a command. He goes down at the end. Note to self: always go down at the end of questions.

> HUSBAND: Yeah, definitely. Lots of space for the dogs, and we were thinking of getting some more animals –

> WIFE (corrects): Well, we'd have to consider the renovation costs. And location. I mean, it would be a compromise on the commute.

She looks at *insert husband here*. Not her commute, she means his commute … Jules keeps his eyes on her. He encourages her. He knows it's great TV when the woman speaks for the woman and the man.

Jules always wears a grey suit, like Bruce Wayne, unless the show is somewhere hot and sunny like this Hawaii one. He always stands closer to the camera. He has more hair and is taller than *insert husband here*. Wife is standing between Jules and *insert husband here*. When Wife speaks to Jules her eyes go big and wide like a lamb's. Not like when she speaks to *insert husband here*. Like Fuzzball the lamb, who Ian brought and I helped to feed and look after for a year. I built him a bed using shoeboxes and those edible things you get in packing that look like cereal but taste blah. The cat did not like Fuzzball. Then we ate him. Ian said it was a good thing.

Twat does a wet tut and finally goes back to his texting.

TWAT: Never mind.

It's like the wife wants to have sex with Jules, not her husband. Once, before Mum went away, I listened to her and Ian have sex in the bath. I wanted to tell her I'd found her old wedding album under the television. I crept up near and sat outside the door. Lots of splashing and screeching. I imagined it was Jules in there, from *House in the Country*, with one of the wives, the wife from the episode with the house where they turn the horse stables into a microbrewery. We don't have stables here but we do have animal sheds out the back. The first one is full of garden stuff from when Mum said she was going to fix up the garden. The second shed is full of building stuff. Big powders in big powder bags. All that potential going to waste. It makes me dizzy to focus on the blue lines in the sheds. I need the blue lines to fix this place up properly. Potential, potential, potential. Potential means what it could be like – not what it is – if it got some 'focus, love and attention'. That's why I write at least twice a month to Jules. I always include the sheds that are full of stuff in all my letters to him.

Dear Jules,

Hello I am Dylan. I am writing again because of your great work on House in the Country*. My mum and I are your biggest fans. We seen all your episodes. I am going to wear a cool suit like you and be a TV presenter on* House in the Country *when I grow up. Please will you come. The cat is missing and there is lots of crap everywhere, and the sheds are full of crap, and the bugs have won, and I don't know most of the boys who come and go. We cannot 'maximise the property's potential, potential, POTENTIAL!' on our own. Please help me.*

Thank you.

Please can I have a signed photo.

Dylan again.

If only Ian would watch *House in the Country*. He would see how great this place could be. But he says we can't throw anything out. He says he knows exactly what everything costs. He says he can see the money all over everything, like grime. But there's plenty of space for all of us, he says, if we all get nice and cosy. Since Mum got taken that number can be, like, nine or ten of us. On one condition. They all have to chant for world peace. I don't have to because I'm already enlightened. Ian says twice a day, but most days they get around to it once if they're lucky. Usually before bed. Ian gets us all to breathe really fast too until we're dizzy, and then hold our breaths for ages.

IAN: Tricks bacteria into believing you're a corpse.

I am always the youngest by at least two years, but Ian says I'm old and makes everyone call me Grandad. Everyone else is always at least thirteen or fourteen. Tomorrow is the third of April, I think. My birthday. I turn twelve. They are definitely planning something.

I am nearly twelve but I won't hit puberty for ages. Ian said it's going to make me wait for ages more before I'm a real grown-up. It doesn't matter because when I am, I am going to be a presenter on television. With a nice suit and hair and smile like Jules from *House in the Country*. I will be a TV presenter, but I will have an edge. *House in the Country* is the best home-makeover TV show. It is the best TV show on TV. I am the show's biggest fan and it took me, the biggest fan, to realise that the show is missing something.

I have this thing that I can do, like a pulse that goes around in the background, like my heartbeat. If I concentrate on a room, I see these blue lines running along everywhere, over everything. They make me see what the room needs, design wise. I see it all, behind all the mountains of crap. The blue lines pulse around everywhere and show me the room's perfect outline. Its potential. I'm hoping Jules does not see the blue lines too and keep them secret, otherwise I will not have any edge. The blue lines see the room exactly as it wants to be. I sit down and close my eyes and concentrate on the place where they come from, and they pulse across the room to the speed of my heart. Forming blueprints. The lines go in the shape of the vintage lamp or the Edwardian divan. I can see every piece of future furniture needed through the blue lines.

When I am down the laneway at night, a good distance from the house, I look across at the mountains. The other side of the mountains is the town. And the other side of the town is more land and more people, I wouldn't know. I focus on the blue lines, and they run *aaall* the way to the horizon. They flash and crash with forks of blue lightning. Endless potential …

The lines make everything less good in real life. I don't know if anyone else can do it. I never told anyone about it, but it's cool because, like, I live in the present and the future. Like I have a portal inside myself that goes somewhere else. The lines show me how they want the world to be. Mostly I just ignore them. But they get stronger if I concentrate on one certain spot.

They get excited and show me tricks they learn through me watching *House in the Country*.

Alone, I am useless. I can't even screw in a lightbulb. I am hopeless. I couldn't tell you which magazines go on what towers in the TV room, how to hang a shelf, how to install a vintage wood-burning stove, assemble a multi-tiered indoor copper-cage garden. On my own I couldn't tell you how to turn the loft into a master bedroom, how to build a secret passageway that leads down to the basement space where you keep your wine, where the door is a bookshelf. I am hopeless at having anything the way I want it to be.

Ian let me redo just my room, upstairs. He liked it. I obeyed the blue lines as best I could. I nearly died putting up a valance on the curtain rod. I hung all the pictures I could find in the piles of stuff by the back of the cowsheds. I found an old painting in a broken frame of a crying boy, and a metal sign that says ESSO GREEN TRACTOR VAPORISING OIL. I should not have put that up. When Ian saw it hanging on my wall:

> IAN: I hope you didn't damage that putting it up
> – that is an heirloom!

Ian prefers things sitting on the ground behind the sheds. I shouldn't have put it up, so obvious, because then Ian wouldn't have seen all the space I made, because then he told me he needed my room to store more stuff. He said he has to because he is being paid. Some cancer medicines or something – boxes piled high to my ceiling. One of the boxes fell and broke and this thick green ooze came out of it. That night I told Ian about the green-ooze spill. But he was stoned and watching that stupid ice-skating competition.

IAN: Probably shouldn't be breathing that shit in.

Our house is so dark now during the day. Ian's boxes of shit cover almost all the windows, except the front windows facing out onto the yard. Nobody who drives all the way up here can see all Ian's shit. Ian doesn't want that. And at night it is pitch black. I like it. It is easy to disappear like Bruce Lee. When I need to escape, I run blind down the laneway. After I cross the yard, I cannot see my hands in front of my face. I always stand in the dark listening and feeling for any animals or sneaking footsteps for ages. If you go close you can always hear the hens half-clucking. I play this game until I can't feel my hands. I look across the field at the road and see if I can see car lights coming out this way. Then I squat down low and clench and unclench my bum until I'm warm.

Then I stand up and look at the stars. Out here there is so much sky. When I feel the blue lines and look at the sky it is always blank. No lines. The stars do not need any makeover. They have reached their full potential. They are perfect. Down here it's a mess.

When I beg him to let me redecorate the rest of the house, Ian shrugs like he has no power and says he is storing stuff for friends, who come and go. He wouldn't understand if I told him about the blue lines.

IAN: Buddha says –

BUDDHA: Give, even if you only have a little.

Watching TV, Ian taps the side of his head.

IAN: If you're quiet up here little dude, none of this matters.

Yeah, Ian. Buddha definitely lived up to his knees in filth and shit too.

I am going to tell Ian to tell everyone else NOT to touch my tapes. ON PAIN OF DEATH. When Ian gets home, I will get him to tell them all.

When he gets home, he is drunk. Even if he wasn't holding the massive box of Miller and the six cans of Carlsberg on top, I could still tell. When he is drunk his head goes all big and red and fat. Big bleary eyes, all bloodshot. Whenever Ian calls me Grandad, I call him Bloodshot because his eyes are bloodshot when he's drunk, which is a lot, and the comic-book character Bloodshot always gets his memory erased. But Ian doesn't know that reason. He wakes up and cannot remember what happened the night before. Ian likes it. He says it's good to laugh at yourself. You can always hear Ian's laugh come around the corner before he does.

IAN: … put syrup in their beer. Twat! Take this, take this.

Twat scurries like a roach. He runs the beer to the fridge. All the cronies start coming out of the woodwork.

Ian is also carrying a cat box, a bottle of whiskey and three yellow construction helmets.

> IAN: Those lunatics in Poland. Grandad! And surprise, surprise, he's watching TV. *House in the Country*. Kid is obsessed. I dream that show when I sleep. Hey, Grandad, you'll love this.

He leaps over the armchair and lands on the couch next to me. Puts his huge head in my lap, still holding the cat box. He rattles it, like a yeti.

> IAN: You know those lunatics in Poland put syrup in their beer, Grandad? All kinds of sweet raspberry syrup. That's the next thing you'll be complaining about. First the German bugs and now the Polish beer.

> ME: You had beer, Bloodshot.

Ian's mullet on the couch cushion looks like an old dead squirrel. Like roadkill he pinned to the back of his hat. That's why sometimes I call him Roadkill. But not that often. His beard is nearly grey. He's wearing his old leathery waistcoat and is smiling.

> IAN: Yeah! You want one? Hey, EVERYONE! Scramble, c'mon, look lively.

Ian tells us stories. When Ian tells stories, everybody sits in a circle. About when he was young and he hitch-hiked everywhere. Up the west coast of the You Ess. The stories are funny, but then beer makes them sad.

Like clockwork, around one o'clock he starts talking all sad about his friend called Rudd. Talking slow, staring off. Rudd got electrocuted on some broken power lines. We've all heard the story a thousand times.

Rudd and Ian went around cheating people. They stole a truck off a really old man – one of those old American Chevy trucks – and left him by the side of the road.

> IAN: Hitchhiking had gotten *us* that far – who wouldn't stop to pick up an old man?

Ian likes when you shout out questions. One night I shouted one.

> ME: How'd you end up as an exterminator in Ireland?

> IAN: The bug part is hilarious. The Ireland shit you wouldn't believe. Me and Rudd wanted to make out like we were bug killers. Extermination guys. So Rudd got a van and painted her up, and I'd do the talking. We'd be driving around Capitola getting stoned, going door to door. Bug bombing old ladies' houses with shit from the hardware store! We got so much work, we had to start looking up how to do this shit. And there's a science to it. A terrible, terrible biased science, but a science nonetheless. Getting rid of little bugs just going about their day. It's not easy. But if you got 'em, you got 'em.

Rudd was mixed up in all kinds of shit – drugs, gangs. They say he died jumping out of some moving truck but that is total … bullshit.

When the stories slow down, I watch *House in the Country*, but with the sound down because Ian is making Twat play different rock and roll – Jimi Hendrix and Led Zeppelin guitar music. Some of the boys sway from side to side, like river reeds. I do not like the sound of it. When the music is on and he is very drunk, Ian rolls around on the floor. Over old foil barbecues, really old pizza boxes, pieces of plastic sheeting, loads and loads of empty Mr Freeze wrappers and Dunnes large cheese and onion crisp packs. They are my favourites. Ian rolls around when the drink has slowed him down, pinching and tickling boys' legs that go by.

IAN: Tee hee. Tee hee.

TWAT: Sounds like bullshit, Ian.

Ian does not stop tickling ankles or look up.

IAN: What did you say?

TWAT: That your friend … Rudd, the way he died. Sounds like it was bullshit.

Then Ian leaps to his feet. He can fair move when he wants to. He stands over Twat like a giant. A giant yeti. Twat shrinks into the armchair.

A long silence passes. *Ffffff. Fffff, ffffff.* Ian stands there looking down at Twat. Who just looks back at him and pretends to not care. So obvious. Ian is grinding his heel into a flat plastic two-litre Coke bottle. Someone throws a slipper and hits Ian on his right jeans leg.

> IAN: What do you know about it? You wouldn't know bullshit if someone came up and slapped it in your little face.

Ian grabs an old slice of pizza from the table in front of the TV and forces it down Twat's mouth.

> EVERYONE: EAT IT! EAT IT! EAT IT!

All of us get up.

The more Twat groans the more we all laugh. But Twat ruins it before the end by stopping groaning and joining in. Like he's enjoying it. My side is killing me. We all love it when Twat is like a twat. That's our favourite. It is so funny.

Ian picks me up off a filthy flat cardboard box. My eyes are tearful from laughing. Ian licks my face.

> IAN: Ew, salty. Now who's Mr Bloodshot? And you stink – get upstairs and take a bath right now, mister. You stink like dead cat. You haven't washed in weeks. Hey! I have an idea. The lieutenant takes a bath, and you'll all chant! Chop chop. Now. Come on, get the drums, start moving. We gotta do our bit, guys. Grandad! Before you go, take the cat box up to the bathroom.

> ME: Why?

IAN: I don't know why – just because.

First, I do a piss in the broken toilet. Fuck Ian if he wants me to have a bath. I'm going to piss in this toilet because the flusher is broke. I pierce a small floating shit with my piss laser to smell if it's mine. 'Cos if it is, it's been there for ages.

If I play the game where I scratch the back of my hand now, I can do it way past where it hurts. It stops the hurt with pain. For a while. It's toughened up and scabbed. Twat dragged me inside once to show Ian and he poured some dark liquid on it and it stung so good I couldn't see for fifteen hours. Maybe ten minutes. Then I wiped it all over my face and it stayed on way longer than fifteen hours. I looked like a black boy from a war in Africa. I bared my teeth through my arms in the broken toilet mirror and at Action Man.

Next to the broken cabinets, all the lino on the floor is cracked and coming up. It's in a square pattern but it's not coming up in squares. It makes me angry. It's coming up in all different shapes.

Ian calls the toilet wallpaper Sunset Yellow – you can only see it above the ring of dark black mouldy stuff that has gone almost bath height up the wall. My piss is sunset yellow. The bath is dark blue. Cracked along the front. As it fills, I am annoyed at Action Man for being empty. No suds. I piss a few drops on the floor. The bath taps are not broke but the toilet and the sink taps are. The cat box sits on the one space of lino on the floor that doesn't have stuff on it – next to the bath.

Me and Action Man float in the tub.

I hate taking baths. You just sit there boiling in filth. Through the bath I can feel them all downstairs. Clattering around, still moving stuff. Making a circle. Boxes of stuff falling over and them shouting 'Timber!' and laughing. One of them finds the big bongo drum. I hope Ian found no candles. For ages I was sad that I would die in a fire from smoke inhalation and never get to present a show on television. Sometimes I wonder if I did but haven't noticed. Twat and the cronies sit and chant downstairs.

> Hare Hare, Hare Krishna, Krishna Krishna, Hare Hare!

> Hare Hare, Hare Krishna, Krishna Krishna, Hare Hare!

They sound like bullying. Their voices buzz up through the bath. Some of them are so braindead they keep messing it up. They can't get it right.

I splash and sprinkle water over my head. I make fountains. I breathe deep again and again and again to drown out their noise. Drown out the World Peace. They get louder and louder, they are shouting.

> Hare Hare! Hare Hare! Hare Hare!

I can't hear Ian's voice. It is horrible. I plunge my head under the water and stare up at the ceiling and ignore the blue lines. There's a browny-reddy stain on the ceiling that could be blood. Looks like it seeped through from the attic. I wonder if it's where the cat got put. I imagine a tidal wave of blood flying through the portal of the stain on the ceiling. Pouring down on me and quickly filling up the whole bathroom and then the whole house and then washing them bastard hippies and the mould and the roaches and all the mountains of crap out my front door into the yard. It would be great if it happened one day before Jules comes, so we don't have to sleep for ages in the animal sheds. I imagine it again and again. Then again, but this time as human shit pouring out of the browny-reddy cat stain. My tummy rumbles. Maybe my stomach hasn't fully settled.

Suddenly under the water the drumming seems way louder. I stay under. My lungs shrink. I feel the door open.

TWAT (heard from underwater): We were knocking – why didn't you say anything?

I pop up out of the water panting. I grab Action Man as cover. His head is a lid. He has been empty ages. He is all slimy.

Twat asks can he stay and sit on the bathroom floor but Ian is, like, No, fuck off.

I used to play with him as real Action Man in secret, even though he was way bigger against my wrestling figures Hulk Hogan, the Ultimate Warrior and Jake the Snake Roberts. Action Man was the ultimate baddy hulk at the end of the round that they had to kill.

I remember Mum scrubbing me. She would hiss, 'Bad things. Always in threes.' She always scrubbed me raw with an old flannel. We had way less stuff then. Then she'd storm out of the toilet and go shouting down the hall.

MUM: Fucking walls are paper!

One time she went down the stairs, out the door, shouting, and left the house. She left me in the bath to finish washing myself. To the pub, usually, she liked to go. Or to her friend Linda's for a few days' rest.

IAN: Hey dude.

I stare straight up at the cat-stain ceiling and think about me and Ian and Twat, and we are trying to barricade the door shut to protect the rest of the rest of the house from all the blood coming gushing down. The blood is rising past the mould line.

The door closes. Twat is gone. Ian speaks slow, to where you can hear the breathing inside his chest.

IAN: Poor little Twat. Doesn't realise that power corrupts. He knows you're my lieutenant and he gets territorial, like a hyena. Victim mentality. He resonates at a lower frequency than you and me, but it's not his fault.

Ian taps Action Man.

IAN: What's his name? He needs a nickname, Lieutenant. Looks like something kinda Chicano to me, like Pablo or Ernesto?

He makes Action Man bob like a man-of-war from that TV show *Mighty Ships*. The harder he taps, the harder Action Man bobs back to defend.

> IAN: Oh, shit, I bought you that! And not for nothing. You stank to high heaven, boy. She never came near you with soap in your life. You and this tough guy are still friends? I think that's really cool, man. He shall remain nameless – how we're born, and how we die.

The first huge hairy leg comes over the side.

> IAN: Your mother and I agreed on that, once upon a time… That's the Ireland part of the story, shit you wouldn't believe!

Then the other.

> IAN: Been a while for me too. Awwwwww, that is the perfect temp.

Ian nearly empties the bath he's such a yeti. He finally relaxes in but down the tap end of the bath.

> IAN: I miss the light in here, Lieutenant. I think you got a point. You know, I think this house has got real potential. We'll get those brats to earn their keep, do some work around here.

I am staring at the stain and holding my breath because the blood flood is up to the ceiling. He stretches his legs down my side and splashes himself in the face.

IAN: Soon as we've got some extra money, we'll get rid of those ugly old floors. Your mom put that lino everywhere, except where we goddam need it. Start from the bottom. We'll sweep the place for bugs. Properly, not like me and Rudd! Get some good storage. And we only keep what we need. Like this cool guy.

Ian reaches for Action Man. His willy sticks out of the water like a periscope in that TV show *Mighty Submarines*.

IAN: I still think it'd be good to give this guy a name – something tough, right? Like …

I bare my teeth and hiss at him, like a chimp. Slipping and sliding up the non-tap slanty end.

IAN: Hey, hey, hey easy. It's OK, little man. Town is big enough for the both of us. For the three of us, I should say.

He leans forward. My chest is burning from holding my breath from before the hiss. I try to suck air but can't.

The cat box sits empty on the carpet next to the bath. I miss the cat really, really bad. So bad. Like, why didn't I look for her after she disappeared? She must be buried under something. Or Mum stuck her upstairs in the attic ages ago. I fed her for years, and she purred on my legs and let me scratch her behind the ears.

IAN: We're all just Buddhas in the seed, man. Buddhas in the seed.

The back of my neck is pinching like the day I stomped some of Hooty's family. That was a rare sunny one. My eyes roll back in my head and my body goes limp as I levitate upwards. Out of the bath. Straight for the browny-reddy stain. My right arm thrusts out forward like Superman, or smiling Jules when he's leading the couple into the best room in the house. I slip through the stain and up into the attic. My little kitty is lying there.

CAT: Miaow, miaow.

In a pool of moonlight. Miaowing into a little pool of blood because some sharp thing is stuck in her paw. I peek back down into the bathroom – Ian hasn't even clocked that I'm gone – and I shuffle over to the kitty on my knees. I remove the sharp thing in her paw. It was a splinter of attic wood. Ouch, pesky. She gets up. She has a little limp but she hobbles over and *purrrrrs* against me. She does a figure of eight between my legs. I hold her for a while and she lets me. I never knew there was a skylight up here. Her fur is soft – I haven't felt it for ages and ages. Since Mum was here. I'm sorry I neglected you for so long, Cat. When you're better, I'm going to get you a beautiful house made out of wood, with the big cat scratch barrel, and whenever you want you can sleep with me in my bed. No one else owns you now except me.

My eyes snap open and Ian is roaring, splashing and spluttering out of the bath.

IAN: Ugh! You disgusting little – UGH!

He's furiously wiping at himself. I look into the water. I have shit myself pretty bad. Worse than the day before yesterday. That wasn't purring. Action Man floats and bobs in hundreds of nuggets of dark water. He looks sad. Ian is trying to get the sinks to work. I let him work that one out on his own.

IAN: You and this place and everything in it, you fucking disgust me!

Someone is knocking on the door.

IAN: Fuck saaaake.

Ian is gagging. His legs are all shitty and wet. He is flailing around like he's been electrocuted. Sissy. I stay in the water – it's not cold yet – look straight ahead and try not to shiver as best I can. Like a statue. More knocking on the door from outside. Ian washes his crotch using the toilet water and makes more silly gagging sounds. Twat comes in and takes in the scene.

TWAT: What the f–?

The shit and the watery pools on the floor and the cat box on its side and Ian sitting the wrong way on the toilet splashing water on his willy and balls. I am still looking straight ahead.

IAN: Get out! Fuck off.

I notice they've stopped drumming downstairs. Enough world peace for one night. When you get used to an annoying noise, like a car alarm going off for ages, and then it stops, it feels so nice.

I sit in the bath and don't get out because if I get out I have to deal with moving and I have to go check if it really is the cat who made that stain …

Ian almost doesn't say anything until:

> IAN: Tomorrow, boy, you will be cleaned. If I have to put you under the power hose.

He slams the door really hard behind him. I just sit there for I don't know how long. I am annoyed at Ian because of how cold it's getting, and because I can't stop hearing the drumming even though it's gone away. After ages, I play this game where I'm in a meadow in the fresh air. And then I walk by some cows, and they're the ones causing the smell. And another game where Jules Dixon walks into the toilet, right arm outstretched, followed by a little couple who look around the room. Me in the bath. The cat box. The broken toilet. The sunset yellow. The mould. Moment of truth – Jules bites his lip. The couple look at each other, all wide eyed, and then they nod, without saying anything. The wife gasps with happiness, and she hugs *insert husband here*. They can't help themselves – they've found exactly what they were looking for. Jules flashes his signature smile to camera which means …

> JULES (smiling): We've got a sale!

We've got a sale! We've got a sale! We've got a sale! We've got a sale! We've got a sale! Then I come rocketing out of the bath because I can't sit still any more. The blue lines are pulsing. They're insisting, even though I'm not even focusing on their spot. I can see them brighter when I close my eyes. They're not where they usually are. They've come up to the front uninvited. Now if I ignore them, they make my head pound. I run across the landing, shivering head to foot. I slip at the top of the stairs, either on my wet feet or on the blob of salad cream that's been there for ages and won't go away. My wet arse bumps down half the steps, then I bounce right back up onto my feet, not missing a step. It hurt but it was fun. Like I'm in a waterpark. My legs are covered in shit. Everyone is asleep, crawled back into the woodwork. The downstairs stinks of old sweat.

The blue lines pulsate around the room. They make the furniture scream – not through my ears, through my body. I roll around on the couch to get the shit off, and shake myself from side to side to ease some of the pressure. When I shake around it helps to get it out all at once. I had this once before, when I was little. It made Mum cry when I had to get it out all at once, so I learned how to dribble it out. Bit by bit. But it won't work this time. It's so annoying because this is the perfect time to watch that episode of *House in the Country* that Twat and Ian distracted me from today. Even the bugs are asleep. But I can't sit still.

Must prepare. So much to do. I am so behind the lines.

The fresh air helps my head so I put Ian's wellies on. I walk out the yard and down the lane. Someone took the bins all the way out to the roadside. That's rare. Definitely wasn't Twat. He won't go near as far as the road. He says the pylons are giving us all ass cancer.

At the end of the lane, sticking out of the bins, I see these other squiggly black lines, not blue. Big squiggles of shiny bushes, sticking out of the bins in the moonlight. I kick and pull at them. I do not know that it's tape until the cassette falls out: DO NOT TAPE OVER. ON PAIN OF DEATH.

My *House in the Country* tapes. All thirty-two of them. Tape all pulled out.

I tip the bin over to see what I can salvage. An unopened letter from the bottom of the bin is stuck to the top of the tape. Addressed to … me?

I tear it open.

> *Miranda Gerald*
> *Crystal Ball Productions*
> *Great Benedictine St Office*
> *Bristol*
> *15 January 2008*

Dylan
The Wysts
Carthey Rd
Knockfarran
Co. Wicklow

Dear Dylan, Veronica and family,
*   This letter confirms the interest of Channel 3's* House in the Country *in your home as a potential candidate on the show! Congrats!*

We received Dylan's charming letters – he is a very insistent young man. He writes very fondly and sweetly of you, Veronica. You must be very proud. He is very creative. We look forward to meeting him. Having confirmed your address and surrounding land, we see huge potential for transformation. Dylan mentioned lots of 'crap' in his letter? We are very intrigued and would love to see some reference pictures. Could you send them to us at the email address below?

We would like to nominate 7 April as a potential date for our research team and me to pay a visit to allow us all to make acquaintance, get a sense of your home, and discuss further.

Please call or email below to confirm you received this letter, and that 7 April is a workable date. Potential, potential, potential!

Thank you, and very much looking forward to seeing your home.

Warm regards,
Miranda Gerald
Researcher, House in the Country
Ph. 01176453213
E: miranda@hinthec.co.uk

Haitch in the See dot co dot you kay. Miranda Gerald. Just a few dots and letters away.

The seventh of April – that's only a week's time. Five days.

If we are on the show, she can give me more tapes. Not ones taped over a hundred times – nice professional new ones with cases on. And I will hide them really well and sleep with them next to me.

I have to prepare. Maybe Jules will come. I need a clean suit. I hope my stomach has cleared up by then. It would be like a dream to meet Jules and be on the show. We have a reason to clean up now. Ian is going to be so pleased.

My heart explodes and my head flies back and shakes from side to side. I scream but silent. Trying to get it all out. I grit my teeth and hop from one foot to the other.

I carefully fold the letter and sneak back home. I shove an old calendar of George Michael under the front door to wedge it open so I have a clear run out into the yard. The cat comes running in under my feet – thank God, hurray! We brought her back to life!

She, or he, I don't know, I don't think it's our full-time cat, disappears into the kitchen. Maybe she will catch a mouse. I run into the kitchen to give it a cuddle but she runs off. Bitch. I down two big bowls of water from the sink. I spill some on the floor. I have to remember that I did a spill because there's no time to find a cloth to mop it up.

I creep upstairs into Ian's room. The smell of copper coins. I tiptoe up next to Ian, on the other side of Twat. Obviously. I find Ian's shorts on the floor. I love when I find them heavy with stuff in the pockets. I take Ian's phone. I know his passcode because sometimes he makes me do the music.

IAN: I do *not* want to hear a peep of silence, DJ Gramps! Triple Oh Seven, that's the code, and I want ROCK ROCK ROCK – you hear?

I steal the five euro out of his wallet and his lighter. I leave the coins. Twat's eyes open.

TWAT: Your mother didn't die, she abandoned you. Now get out.

I go hide in my room behind the boxes full of green ooze, where I can concentrate on writing the letter back to Miranda and Jules. To distract myself from the blue lines, I pick at the toughened scab on the back of my hand. I gnaw at it with my teeth until it hurts enough to outdo the headache, then I concentrate on what to say. Make it like it's from a grown-up. But who?

To: *miranda@hinthec.co.uk*
From: *Iandahumanbein@hotmail.com*
Hello this is Dylan's mum, Veronica. Seventh of April is great. We will prepare. No ref pictures sorry. See you then.
Veronica and Dylan

I creep downstairs to look for kitty in the TV room. Looking at it from the stairs, it is the TV room I have known all my life. Me and Mum built forts out of the couch cushions to keep out intruders in front of *House in the Country*. Forts like the one in my bedroom upstairs. But now it's different. The blue lines make the TV room not half as good, but that's OK. Because it will be. Once it's reached its potential. I spy with my little line … a future chandelier?

Everyone will know it as well as me, soon, the way it wants to be. I have to prepare the house, one room at a time.

I pick up the first box of magazines I can grab and throw it out into the front yard. The rain is spitting. So little time. If I can get just the TV room done by dawn then Ian and them will see and join in and help me do the rest. I run back and forth and back and forth and the rain picks up speed. I am getting soggy. I lug out years of mountains of stacked-up crap. Every box makes my head lighter. The blue lines ease off to a level a bit less painful. There are noises coming out of me I've never heard before.

I lug twenty-five boxes outside without stopping. Boxes of old lighters, boxes of broken lunchboxes, boxes of loads and loads and loads of coat hangers. Loads and loads and loads of rude magazines. One box was full of dead stuffed animals. Taxi-something. When I see an enemy cockroach, I say take that! And ha ha to all the creepy crawlies. And I am sorry for taking away your house in the country. Then I bare my teeth and make my eyes wide open. Like the scary dragon-head statues with big tongues in Bruce Lee films. Then the roaches usually run away unless they're big like Hooty. Then you have to squash them.

I scrape the bits of shit the couch missed off my middle. It doesn't matter because it has to go too. There's no way Jules would want to keep the couch. It's old and rotten and covered in shit – along with almost everything else. I find an old, tall lamp hiding in the corner that I never knew was there. It has no bulb. But it's rustic. Since the blue lines just track around it, that must mean the lamp should stay. I'm keeping the old video player, and television and where I watched all of *House in the Country*. I am not turning it into a fish tank. Though I would if Jules says.

Outside I leap up onto the soggy crap mountain. It's like a load of hay bales. I start lighting her but it's a fucker because it's coming down cats and dogs and nothing's catching. But a good dart of one of them fluids from the shed and she goes *woof*. It goes up so quick it knocks me off. The flames go mad high really fast. The fire feels nice. It stops me shivering. I stand there and play a game. I am Jules, my right arm outstretched. I am wearing a very expensive suit made from crocodiles. I present the whole episode of our house in the country.

> ME (as Jules): A big fire – great for mould! – which you can easily keep going with the stuff in this bottle called isopro– pol.

I'm so excited for the future. The blue lines are so reliable now that you can see them all the way to the horizon. Big crashes and forks of lighting. Thanks to Ian.

I keep lugging. I've barely made a dent. I don't know how big Miranda's research team is going to be – there might be twenty of them. Box after box after box goes up on the fire. Then clothes, food trays, old newspapers, binders with papers and shit that no one gives a shit about any more. Shit that doesn't deserve to exist. Once it's gone Ian won't care. He'll be happy. He'll like the more space. He'll feel like a huge weight has lifted. He said himself he misses the light that's getting clogged up inside the house.

The flames lick up mad high. A thousand feet in the air. Cat is sitting just inside the front door. She sits very still. She is looking at me.

CAT: You're in deep shit, pal.

I try be psychic and tell her inside her brain.

ME (to cat): Everything is going to be better off once I've made the room like it is in my head.

I run past Cat and kick the door to give her a fright because she tried to get me to abort my destiny. She moves away and that makes me feel happy but only a tiny amount of the happy compared to seeing her alive earlier.

I flap around like a firebird because I can hear birds singing in the trees. Either it's near dawn or they think it is because of the fire. Either way, the more company that's not the cat the better.

The couch is the last thing. I drag it outside and the roaches run everywhere. I lug it close to the fire, then lift the far end over so the couch cartwheels into it. I pat it like an old horse.

ME: Bye, couch. You were a good couch.

It lies sleeping on the fire. It burns really slow and so I get sick of it.

Next job is the lino. Mum would be upset, but once she sees it with the makeover, she'll be over the moon.

The videos live in my head because I remember what Jules said when his jacket was off and his sleeves were rolled up.

> JULES: To remove old lino is tricky. You need to heat it and scrape it. Heat and scrape.

I creep upstairs quietly. It would be a disaster if they all woke up before I was finished. The toilet stinks something rotten. I do not want to see into the bath. I frown at the floor and hiss air out until I get the hairdryer.

I heat and scrape at the lino in the kitchen. I'm panting and it's slow work – I've only had a few large bags of Dunnes cheese and onion and shook out the toaster crumbs twice in the past few days. Cat comes out from behind something. She likes the heat, the warmth from the hairdryer. Her fur is so soft. Sweet, fluffy kitty.

I wake up with a start on the kitchen floor to the whole world shaking. The sun coming through the back door has me dying of thirst. I must've been out for ages. I sink two bowls of water. I am still holding the hairdryer. I can hear Ian coming down the stairs. He has seen the fire ring in the yard. I go running out the back door and sneak around the long way towards the front yard.

All Ian's little shit rat cronies, whose heads I want to stomp into the burnt ground, sit around the big fire ring – stomp them until they're blood and dust – sunbathing and drinking coffee and laughing where I burned all

Ian's stuff. They are waiting for him to wake up. They do not want to miss the show. I hide behind the sheds and watch.

IAN: Twat! Get –

Twat sneaks up and grabs me all snidey from behind. His hands feel cold and clammy. I can't breathe. I try to whack him in the balls with the hairdryer plug. He's six years older but he is still afraid of me. He drags me out and throws me in the fire ring. Ian stands at full height. His eyes are the most bloodshot I've ever seen. They are as red as the rest of his face.

IAN: You did this because I destroyed your TAPES?

ME: Because the *House in the Country* team are coming, Jules and Miranda. They're coming! To help us.

IAN: Twat, grab him.

Twat gets me in a headlock.

IAN: If you're going to behave like an animal, you'll be punished like one.

Twat points a thumb behind himself.

TWAT: Orderly queue!

IAN: Hold him down.

Two of them pin my arms and legs to the burnt ground.

IAN: You dung beetle. You rat. You want your breakfast? Here have your breakfast. Do it boys – not on his face.

And all the cronies make a circle and piss on me. It is hot and because I struggle some of it dribbles into the bottom of Ian's wellies. I am sad because their piss probably broke the hairdryer. The only thing in the house that works ...

IAN: You made me do this, Dylan. When you behave like a fucking animal, you will be treated like one. When you behave divinely, you will be shown divinity.

Twat can't piss – what a twat. We all laugh. Except Ian. Twat is holding his shrivelled willy and nothing will come out of it. He's trying so hard. We all laugh at him.

ME (with everyone): HA HA, HA HA, HA HA!

IAN: You owe me, and several partners of mine, several thousands of euro. You're going to be working, boy. Twat, I want to be able to see my face in that boy. Even if you have to use the hose.

Days go by. I sleep as much as I can to get closer to April seventh. I snuck George Michael Calendar up to my room to keep track, even though he's a different year and the days are all different. March George wears sunglasses and sits by a swimming pool. Note to self: swimming pool.

When me and Action Man and George Michael Calendar go to sleep, we all go on *House in the Country* together. Jules is leading the three of us around our house. There are plants in big pots inside. The attic is converted to a vaulted upstairs ceiling. There are new sash front windows for lots of light. Ian is rolling his eyes, but happy. There's a wood-burning stove where my tapes used to be. Above that is a new flat TV, attached to the wall, which is wired up to the video player. The kitchen has a marble-topped island. All of the cupboards are old, distressed wood. Some of the art is a bit crap. We will sell it after Jules and the team are gone. A few nights ago, Macho Man Randy Savage came on the tour. But he was very quiet – he barely said anything. Him and Jules couldn't see each other, so I'm not sure where he was.

I lie in bed curled in a ball. I shut my eyes, hard as they can go. But I can barely sleep. The blue lines pound in my head. My secret edge. I am so excited about my future. I can't help looking at Action Man and George Michael Calendar and thinking that bad things don't come in threes, good things do. If it goes well, then they'll give the house a makeover and Mum will come back. That's three. We cannot miss this opportunity.

It's the night before April seventh and I cannot sleep – like Christmas, only real. I can't lie still. Any scraps of paper I find I draw what the lines want so I can share the ideas with Miranda. Nothing can go wrong tomorrow. The lines are so excited. They're pounding so loud I can't hear my heartbeat. They drag me out of bed. They're doing something different. They're pulling me now, not pulsing. I take Action Man as backup and leave George Michael Calendar to hold the fort and defend against any intruders.

I creep downstairs, past the blob of salad cream.

Bloodshot snores on floor pillows. He has been drowning his sorrows. Twat is curled up beside him like a worm. This room is so big without all the crap.

The blue lines flash around Ian's snoring face. Little crashing forks of lightning. His mouth hangs open and drools down his beard. He sleeps at a forty-five-degree angle. The TV is on mute, on the blue menu screen.

I close my eyes and stare at Ian as hard as I can, close enough to hear his breathing in his chest. The lines make a box shape. The cat box!

I run upstairs and bring it down. I lower it carefully onto Ian's head but it's the wrong shape. It's too small.

ACTION MAN: No, dummy. *House in the Country!* Remember?

Action Man shows me how a few times then I sit him down quietly on the old farmhouse table with a good view. Twat sleeps like a twat. I have to stop myself from sniggering out my nose.

I slowly tilt the big TV. Hooty makes a run for it. The coward. Teeth bared and clenched like a chimp, I hoist it up over my head.

TWAT (whispers): Do it.

Jesus!

ME (whispers): Wha'?

TWAT (whispers): Do it. Please.

So annoying. Because Twat has said to do it, it makes me not want to now. But my arms are shivering under the weight. I can't hold it up any longer.

ME: Potential, potential, potential!

BANG! I haul the TV down screen first on Ian's head. It makes *such* a loud noise! Good thing we're in a house in the country. There's no one for miles. Crashing blue sparks and little flames fly out of him. TV-Head-Ian wriggles and tries to get to his feet but the TV is electrocuting him.

TV-HEAD-IAN: *PHRRRRWWWWWRRRR!*

Ian the big TV-Yeti gropes for something, someone to help. Twat gets a mop to hit him with.

TWAT: Fuck you! Fuck you!

Ian flops up and down from the waist. It's so silly, like he's doing the worm upside down. Makes me laugh. Me and Twat jump back when the blue and red sparks jump out at us like electric roaches. TV-Head-Ian flops a bit more, then stops flopping.

He said I should use the TV for something useful. Just as long as I plug it out first … Oops.

I stick Ian's wellies on. They're my wellies now –
I'm keeping them. Out in the yard, I look at the sky for
some light relief. No lines. Calm. The sky is the limit
now. And beyond!

I wriggle my head and throw my hands in the air. I
can't wait for tomorrow. I'm so excited about my future.
I will do anything for Jules. He'll understand the lines
once he sees proof of my edge. Then I will become a
big TV presenter like on *House in the Country*.

NO FRILLS

Written in No Frills

WALKIN AROUND THE BIG NO FRILLS, taste of metal
… Dandrin. Dandrin around, wonderin is life enough,
adventurous enough. Does it matter after death? Does
death hold any hope of adventure? … Dandrin, under
some trash from the charts, fizzin and pipin through
the tannoy above … What does it say about your life
if you're hopin for adventure in death? … For a while,
lookin for an acceptable piece of fish, but doubtful in
here. Standin, starin in the canned foods aisle … Does
it make me ill in the head or right in the head? Don't
be slingin diagnoses around. The hangin fluorescent
ceilin light is high-pitched hummin …

Wish I'd my sunglasses on, to be dandrin …

Into the frozen food section. To find some fast-
frozen bollocks, and I'm, laaak, go on then, so I dander
around the big long vat, and the shrimps catch my eye.

I like a shrimp. Thinkin about them on top of the bean, noodle, few other veg thing in the saucepan at home. Heat that up in the pan, throw a few shrimps on it, all fried widabidda butter on 'em, and a few other nicey spices, and Bob's your uncle. And everyone else is just … Dandrin around. Pickin their groceries.

Beside me? They're just … Walkin around. In another dimension. If I reached out and touched them, would they be solid? They'd be freakin. They all frown down at the fast-frozen fish. Concentratin. Like their brow is a small activated shield. Like their brow is the heel of a foot but on a face.

The main brand in the big shrimp vat is called Anchor's Bay. Lovely anchor on the pack. A picture of a little island with a lighthouse and a body of water stretchin off. A vision of peace. Lovely and islandy. You can taste the sea salt in the back of your throat. They catch lobsters and all that shit out there in East Canada. Anchor's Bay is a fisherman's town from a storybook.

Turnin the bag of frozen shrimps around, but slowly so as not to wake them, it says – Anchor's Bay, registered to a factory address in Quebec City. And under that it says in big capitals – PRODUCT OF CHINA.

All along the vat in all the trays, there's loads of bags of different Anchor's Bay mollusc products. The shrimps are cold, they're hurtin my hand. The next Anchor's Bay molluscs I'm pickin up is a pack of pre-cooked mussels, a rectangular one like a cold brief-case with a plastic laminate window. And this one says – PRODUCT OF CHILE.

I rock back on the heels of my soggy house shoes – somethin's leakin out of the vat – and frown down at the mussel-meat briefcase. The farm in faraway Chile drifts into my mind. Back where the mussels still have their shells. Rows of men are shuckin like lightnin, shovellin loads and loads and loads of them out of a big pile into boxes, like somethin not alive.

Next one I pick up is a pack of crabsticks, which says – PRODUCT OF THAILAND. And then the next pack says – PRODUCT OF ECUADOR. I'm clutchin the molluscs in a pink grip. I don't know where to look. I'm laughin way too hard for No Frills. It hits me like a golf club in the mouth where I am: in a giant yellow shoebox borne aloft by thousands of souls around the world. Dandrin, in the horn of the yellow pyramid, and *this* is how they chose to decorate the place? This is the house they chose to build, taking into account the back-breaking, behemoth sacrifice it requires for it to exist at all? To bring all of us frowners these low, low prices?

Dandrin back, up along the big vat.

Wild Caught Shrimp (Easy Peel) 9,97$. Cooked shrimp 8,97$. Basa Fillets 5,75$. King Crab Legs 3,97$, Canadian! Jesus …

The selection is endless.

Canadian Jesus … What would he look like. Probably big. Broad shouldered and jawed and toothed, like a hockey player. But in white robes. Probably a few tattoos. Good low hairline, and obviously white. Like current Swedish Jesus.

These molluscs got to have a much more adventurous life in death. Their corpses got to travel the world. I stifle a giggle, helpless. I wish I'd my fuckin sunglasses because No Frills is makin my frown ache.

Where am I? Where are we? Where are you? You all seem so far away. You used to be nearer, didn't you? Have we always been this way?

I want, at the very least, an adventurous death. After my life is done, my ghost will retrace the molluscs. I'll float along the assembly line of the men who shuck the oysters free of their shells in big chainmail gloves. I'll dander along above the Chilean fishermen as they pull the mussels out of the water and fast freeze them and load them on ships to be hauled over to the Francophones, nearly 11,000 kilometres away. To cook, sterilise and pack them quick in their storybook briefcases.

The strange stink of rot driftin up off the fast frozen. We can all whiff it, together. Alone.

I drop the molluscs and give my pink hand a flickin. My veg-noodle thing will be fine on its own.

No Frills voice pipin, interruptin the pop fizzin over the tin, 'Prices so low, it's embarrassing!'

What's that taste of metal? In here, it feels like somethin's missin. If we're all walkin the same road together, are we each supposed to figure it out on our own? Was I clocked in the mouth with a nine iron?

I spit a bit of metal spit on the floor and am caught red-tongued by a bald fellow wearing his cagoule over his big winter coat. Then once our eyes have met, he shoots his frown back down and grabs hold of two big packets of smoked salmon. His face looks on high alert, holdin them both up and makin them compete. Lookin at them, all serious.

A woman nearby has her foot jammed in one of the big fridge doors, holdin it open. She is holdin two different almond milks. Original and vanilla. Then she lets slip and drops them both like she never wanted either of them anyway. Spilled liquid almonds creep across the floor. The man in the cagoule swivels to see who's makin all the racket, then does a *pssst!* to bring her attention around to what he's holdin – his two salmon hopefuls. She turns, and when she blinks, I notice at the right collarbone of her beige-and-green yoga top there's a large patch of damp. Blinkin once, twice, like she's seen a ghost, her eyelashes are clung together.

He drops the salmon packets back into the vat and pulls the cagoule over his head and unzips and drops the coat and underneath he's wearin ... nothin? Nothin at all?

On his top half. Except small silvery tassels on his nipples, and that glitter that you can tell has been rubbed into his hairy belly from before. He struts around like a cockerel, over to my side of the big vat, where I see his glittery boots with the big Cuban heel, over dark-purple corduroy trousers tucked in. His wrists shoot up in the air and his body convulses like the family-dinner scene in *Beetlejuice*. Like he's surprisin himself with his own jerkin. He shimmies his tits, and the almond-milk lady marches off to complain, or just get in her car and leave.

He knocks over a big pyramid of toilet rolls. He's havin anxiety sweats under his pits and down his back, which makes his body glitter sparkle even brighter under the fluorescents.

I can't take my eyes off him. They're burnin into his sweaty, hairy back and bingo wings. Someone twisted his clockwork wind.

Oops, there go a stack of toilet ducks, waddlin across the floor.

Almond-milk woman comes back and eyes him. Her jaw is clenched. Her eyes are on fire, throwin looks down a load of different aisles for a member of staff. She sees me, fast frozen to the spot, eyes gripped, starin. I can't stop. She's posturin, tryin to pluck up the courage to say somethin, when Tassel Man spins round and we lock eyes on the shimmy.

'Simple now, drop! Widda buggay.' His jiggerin is all out of time with the insert-pop-music-here tinnin over the tannoy. He sticks his tongue out and blows raspberries. He kicks his legs up in the air like an exotic dancer from the Crazy Horse in Paris, and the shiny boots are sparklin under the low overhead LEDs. One of his heels skitters in a pool of defrosted something, oozin out of the leaky vat.

He's out of breath. I reach out and catch him by the wrist to steady him from fallin. His hands are dry … So it wasn't anxiety sweatin – he just had too much caffeine or somethin?

He and I alone again, in the fast-frozen-food section. He's clasped on to my hand pretty tight. I stifle a laugh and send him a wave of warm-hearted goodness through his hand. I don't know if I'm capable of doin that but I feel grateful enough to him to give it a go. A story would help, but I can't think of one. I can never find that place in my mind with a million stories when I need to, to whisk him away to a distant land across the sea. If only I'd a hook to snag one.

Then it comes to me. 'Let's stow away! Me and you and your purple boots. Down in the belly amongst the cargo. We'll set sail at Anchor's Bay and jump ship at the first port. We'll be shipwrecked in the land of the molluscs, and be tied up on spits. And just before our darin escape, as we go round and round over the gatherin fire, the molluscs will encircle us with spears, clackin an old sea shanty, "Clack, clack-clack-clack-clack". An ancient song clacked since always to thank their sea gods for such a generous catch. They'll be jabbin at us on the spit as we sweat, soon to be cooked and suited and booted and trammelled into our briefcases.'

Throughout my little half-tale, Tassel Man danced around to it like the sea. Embodyin. Crabbin his fingers over his head.

Security man is makin his way down now. A short, tired-lookin pot-bellied fellow, who's lookin a bit cagey, walkin down towards us. God, it's near impossible to get kicked out of these places. And I don't want this fella to be kicked out, but … eh, he's causin a bit of a ruckus. Things will be back to normal after he's gone.

I give him a cursory nod and a pat on the bare shoulder – 'You'll be all right, mate' – and hope that helps him. Off he goes, mostly of his own accord, still dancin and thrustin his wrists up to the sky. Everyone ignores Tassel Man, dandrin out the exit into the lot, carryin his winter coat and cagoule in a ball.

Pickin up one more Anchor's Bay product out of the vat … 'Mélange de Fruits de Mer', that's what a seafood medley's called in French Canada.

SCAB

Written on Thames Path, near Kew Green, London

OUT THE FRONT OF THE GARAGE, I tore this big scab off my leg for the pain it would cause me, but instantly resented the future itch it would cause me, because that would mean the pain was drawing to its end.

It made use of the whole top of my right leg, down to the territory of my kneecap, and had crept up to where the hair of my treasures kicks off.

It bled like a fountain. Not a fountain. More like someone stuck me with fifty of them drawing pins I used in my bedroom wallpaper. See, this scab wasn't your average – it was deep yellow with purple rivers of lava running through it.

So how it happened was like you see in the old comedy skits in black and white, where the obnoxious French waiter with anal posture and an anally twizzled moustache comes in, and the look on his face, like there's a piece of rotting donkey flesh in one of the twizzles under his nostril, but he leaves it there to remind him not to try to be happy. He stalks in quietly with the white towelette over his arm and stiff as a board, like he's holding onto a wet fart. He pinches the edges of the dining cloth between index finger and thumb. The log-cabin dining room falls silent. A small drop of sweat beads above his matted-down-with-oil moustache, betraying him. He takes hold of a sharp breath, concentrating – you could always cut the tension in the air with a knife – then he *whips* the cloth in one, out from under all the dishes, all the lighted candlesticks and the porcelain vases with the flower bouquets, leaving the whole dinner set miraculously intact. Nothing budges from its original position, everyone in the dining room bursts into roaring applause.

So I did that with the scab.

But there was definitely no applause in it, and *I* definitely shook underneath, because I was on bended knee with the right leg stuck out straight on the gravel. My camo combats were bunched around my left ankle, and my sock was sticking out the top of my right boot, and the bit of sock covering my toe was gone thin enough that I could feel winter's fangs biting it. I hate bending over – my spine always threatens to go. And I'd to be swift too because I was running out of time before the lads would be done fixing my bike. She'd been banjaxed since the collision.

First plan was pick-picking slowly all the way around. Nicking gently at the edges of it with the box cutter. Spots of blood, yes, few spots beading to the surface to rub off with my smallest finger, the one with the least muck. I'd to be double swift too, 'cos I was losing the evening light. Careful as a cucumber to keep her intact, I slid two of my fingers in under its right edge and three under the left. Few more beads of blood (nothing compared to what was coming) that dribbled down the sides till I whipped her up quick with all my might. Whipping, whipping it and liiiiiiifting it off until off it came! In one. Aaaaah ...

Now that's better, isn't it? Now, who is boss? Me – and unless you play your cards right, you're homeless, you're a homeless scab.

My leg was shuddering from the severe transition and the blood loss so I lapsed back onto the ground like a crab, and my toe came through the last line of sock.

I lapsed back all cramped, right leg stiff and left leg crumpled underneath. I held it aloft, the scab, trying to ignore my leg. I held it spreadeagled on my hands like the devil's duvet cover, thinking (hoping this was registering on my face), *Yeah, scab, I win, you lose. Don't forget it.* There was a small drop of mesmerisation in there too, but behind that, worry; that I hadn't resurrected whatever gave rise to that bastarding scab in the first place.

In the garage, the lads stopped wrenching and oiling and farting and took notice. One of them roared a string of unrepeatable expletives and went running into the back office, and emerged red-faced with a wad of tabloids that'd last you a whole Christmas worth of fires, and proffered them at me. Two more followed him out.

I barely even registered them, though. I was too busy examining the scab up close and personal.

Soon as it come off, the yellow and the purple rivers began to blacken. The slick side, the side that had been touching my cut, sparkled like petroleum jelly. I wasn't able to get half as close to it before, as it was down on my leg and I never put my spine under undue pressure and don't own a magnifying glass.

The scab had the scaliness of a bog. A Martian bog would be the least worst way I could describe it. Where its surface had crusted over, sealing in a million years' worth of secrets.

The mechanic lads got in at me with the wads of thick tabloids, opening them up and proffering them at me, patting at me and padding, with the headlines roaring 'HOW MANY MORE MUST PERISH? Youth knife gangs out of control', 'WIN A PRIZE DRAW!'

The blood swept into the paper and mixed with the ink, and the only response they could get out of me was the odd grunt from the stinging. It was that class of sting that started to make my thoughts go backwards.

Bloody stuff was sandpaper, not newspaper, until it soaked through the pages. 'MORE MUST PRSH … You knif gns cortl'. 'WN PRZE DRAW!'

As they mopped the blood and covered over the scab's former plot, I rolled it carefully and sweetly, showing it compassion now, like the paradox of what I'd shown it before. I rolled it into a fine roll, as an artist would have to with one of his paintings if he was going on holidays and couldn't do without it.

I slid it down into the side of my backpack, sticking out. That'd have to do until I figured out some other arrangement at home, now that my bike was all oiled and tuned and road-ready once again. I took out some notes from my groin pouch and placed them on the gravel next to me, so the lads knew they were paid.

Their whining noises turned to confusion noises, then they quietened down. I got helped to my feet and, despite the objection, they pulled up my camos.

I'd gone half strange without my bike. It took twice as long as scab forming for the lads to get her fixed.

It was nice to see her good as new. I placed a hand on her saddle in such a way as to make sure she knew that I knew that the scab wasn't her fault.

I limped up onto her and wheeled away into the darkness of the river path home, overgrown with hedge-rows like guards of honour. She purred lightly going over stones and bumps and bits of aul' branch that the river would pull down to be turned into oil in about a million years' time.

If someone gave me a time machine, I wouldn't fanny around in the past going back to visit Caesar, Attila or Genghis Khan. I'd go forward into the future. To lump and roll as many barrels of it back as I could. Get as much out of it as I can, after the whole world's gone fully askew, when it's only the Martians left to pick at our scraps and try and piece us back together.

Under the tabloids, the scab's former plot was crying out for some clean air.

Now and then, I threw my head back to clock its silhouette, to make sure it was still there and I hadn't dropped it on the path only for a dog or a badger to find it the next morning and eat it up for breakfast.

I needed to figure out a better plan than that.

Bump, crack, snap, smoke, smoke, cackle – little lights from some smokes up ahead, past the flicker of her dynamo-powered light on the front wheel. A heron upped sticks and fucked away off, flapping across to the far bank. The birds know all the river's secrets, and they all talk to each other and know when it's best not to stick around.

Smoke, smoke, little red lights, so I slowed her down a touch, until she stopped clattering and bumping so hard on the tree roots.

Flicker, flicker, red smoke coming up in front, quick. Shadows lurking down the shadow path, where only evil shadows would lurk. Their little addictions were a dead giveaway of their positions, though, and their number, and their stronger and weaker arms. I memorised quick.

I clicked her newly liquid gears, hefted her up to the top one so's I could get past the red flickers and get home as quick as I could to figure out mine and the scab's next move. Maybe offer an olive branch, so's the two of us can face the facts and not be all at logger-heads (like whenever I hear that word said, it makes me think of something – one of the skits we watched in the old black and white that were always on just before bed. With the two lumberjacks balanced on the far ends of the trunk of a tree. And they're floating down past the log-cabin dining room on a vast, slow-moving river, must've been somewhere up there in the remote north-west of … America? And they've got their dukes up. Roars of adrenaline! Bursts of applause from across the banks where the other hardy loggers have gathered to a head, clinking bottles and ready for the after-graft entertainment. 'Go on! Splinter him! Stick him! Hold him under and drown him!' Remote north-west of America, or France? But then the beavers start eating the log, and then the two loggers are clutching hold of each other for dear life!), so we could find some common ground between where I was trying to get to and where scab likely saw it going. But I doubted it.

Coming up on the three lads, and I could see no way past. *Hock, spit,* went the top young weasel, and he slammed his hands down on the centre of *my* handlebars. With the fag on, between his index and his middle finger, billowing smoke up into the eye God gave me, and the lungs God gave me. The body He entrusted me with to keep clear and keep away from fraternising with foul lowlifes. His breath was old fags stink. His splotchy hands were all red and all splotchy blue.

Flanked by the other two rats. 'Here, lad! *Tsst.* Giz a look at the bike! That nicked? Looks a lot like my cousin's bike got nicked last week. Giz a go of it.'

His noises were all nasal.

'Get off that bike now, that's my cousin's bike. Now, I won't tell the guards, and you won't end up in that river.' Followed by a string of wretched, unrepeatable expletives.

I took my hands off the handlebars and lowered them slowly down by my sides, still and stony, only just out of reach of the knee pocket of my right camo. And I let nothing on face-wise to betray the little sudden wriggle of activity that could be felt going on in the schoolbag. Stayed stony.

'My cousin stabs lads for way less than this.'

I leaned back to feign fear, as the young fella leaned in far enough so I could see the bristles up his nose.

'Here, lads, he's a cyclops!'

Hyena shrieks and cackling from behind, then SLAP! He sucker punched me across the right side of my face, the side with no eye, no chance to block. This cowardly scum, he put me in mind to mount their three heads, etched in surprise for a million years over my hearth. My heart was pounding in my empty socket, but the slap put me down far enough to get the right leg camo-pocket button unsnapped, and my grip firmed tightly around the handle of the box cutter.

The main weasel bared his crooked teeth and hissed more of his smokey poison at me, drawing wild cries out of the rodents on his flank. He groped and tugged my handlebars, soaking up all her fresh oil.

'Get off. D'you hear me, freak? Get off!'

I gripped a good breath behind my teeth and gripped a firm hold of the box cutter. I shifted my weight and looked kind of down, to make it look like I was conceding and getting off the bike. I slowly put one hand next to his on the handlebar to steady. Focused in, target acquired and locked, and ready to pull just as my bag thrashed open and the scab lunged right out onto the face of the main weasel lad. It wrapped itself around his whole head, cap and all, and up off my handlebars flew his dirty, splotchy hands. He staggered back, fingers flicking and frozen blind, like the dancing chorus girls in the old comedy skits in the black and white, and no doubt if you were betting on the state of his face, you'd bet your house that it was gone all agape. Mine stayed stony. I was at pains to hide showing them my surprise, nor did I want to show Scab I approved.

Scab's scaly surface cracked as it flexed and tightened – beat, stricken gasp, beat and *crack* – squeezing all the disbelief out of him.

The two rodents on the flank ran off, both ways up the river path, screeching applause. The filth.

The lad's body convulsed like he was being defibrillated, then he collapsed back onto the ground. His legs dropped out from under him. Scab, with a fair strength too, rolled him off in under the old elders by the river's edge.

Muffled screams and his legs were still kicking, lepping and rolling like the Tasmanian Devil. Thrashing up sticks and stones, and bits of aul' flattened elderflower heads, aul' cans and faded Twister wrappers. *Thump* (on a root), *whump. Thump* went Scab. *Thump, thhhump.* Then all the kicking and the thrashing stopped dead.

I stood for a while, looking ahead and holding my breath so none more of that disgusting poison snuck its way into my lungs. My eye socket was going *PANG POUNG PANG PAONG PANG PUNG,* and my lungs were burning with stagnant air. Then finally, just with the eye, I swung a glance over to the shadow where my former flesh had dragged your man.

Out peeped Scab, like a grass snake peeping up into the moonlight.

Scab had rolled itself back up the way I'd rolled it, easiest for travel. I looked for a while, and it kept one end raised and stayed still. Unmoving. It stared back for a while, then lowered itself down slow. Then Scab unrolled itself out like a rug, and lay as flat as it could go.

A heron's wings splished and splashed on the river's surface down the way, like a decoy.

I stood there, gripping my handlebars, and after a few spits to purge the smokey filth, I threw a curt nod towards my left shoulder. Quick as a shot went Scab, and scurried up my right camo leg, over the bloody mess it made, and positioned itself back into the bag the way I'd put it in earlier, showing me that it accepted that I am the dominant one of the two, and that I would be dictating terms. Phew. We took a look both ways down the path, and we biked on.

I had some heavy thoughts ... and plans, around the night for as soon as we got in.

That evening, I would allow Scab to be present for my half-hour of exercises. See, when the eye goes, the lid above it gets lazier and lazier and lazier, so you've to keep up the exercises so you don't look to all the world like a total spaz. Having Scab there would motivate me to work harder. To look capable, and show off the fact that I could do more than fine on my own.

Presumably, if it was born of my flesh and blood, then I was its wound too? Was it still here because it thought I needed further repair? Where did it get that idea? And how did it know? Why didn't it just respond to the area that needed healing? Maybe because it thought that if it didn't do anything, things would just get worse.

The other non-worry – well, potential worry, more long term – was what's to say whatever gave rise to Scab in the first place was going to produce another one just like it in the same plot. I'd rip that one off too and then there would be two and one of me. If it happened once, it would happen twice, and if it happened twice, it would happen again, and if there was any flesh left on my leg, then I was facing off against three.

I could stay on the path past the house, and cycle the two of us way into the forest then get separated and leave a different way than the way I brought us in. That would be reckless, to say the least. Because how long would it be before Scab found itself going through somebody else trying to find its way back to me?

If the stepfather was still around, he'd be digging out the rat box. This plastic see-through box filled with water that sat out behind the brambles. It had a trapdoor on top of it made of an X-ray of his own blackened lung. But that would be no use, not a hope. Scab has no breath and could easily lie flat on the surface of any water like a lilo. Not like them poor rats once they fell in. They clambered and gasped over each other and up on each other's backs until they were just floating black lumps.

If I burned Scab in the hearth? If I took it by surprise? But I'd have to grip hold of a fair breath first, or wear a clothes-peg on my nose, because I've no desire to know what my own cooking flesh smells like.

The way he handled that thug, Scab's thirst for blood was clearly as dry as the fire. It was definitely prolonging my life until it could gain in number. I wondered how it planned to kill me ... If I was a gambling man, I'd be lying asleep in bed.

Once we were home and in out of the chill, I got the fire going. Like as always, the first crackles of the wax pinecone began to calm my head. Once I'd the shoes off, the fire levelled me a bit. It put me back in mind to offer Scab that olive branch I was thinking of offering before the attack, but I couldn't think of the right way to go about it.

So I went into the kitchen to bang two ice cubes out of the tray, wrap them in blue roll and put the whole thing into my swollen socket. I felt the cold of it enough to shoot down my legs.

I settled down in front of the TV in my chair. My chair now ... That still entombs him... The stepfather. His breath was always aul' spirits stink.

Sat here by the hearth, watching the old comedy skits in black and white, was the only place I can remember seeing him where he didn't have a look on his face like he wanted to wring your neck.

I got my fair share of hammerings, but at the same time, he was a man who spoke in direct and even terms. He never let me forget the golden rule – to be prepared for Murphy's Law. That it takes toughness to adapt to any change in circumstances. That it's needless to become attached to anything, even your own flesh and blood. But as far as I can remember, scabs never gave me any trouble; they always just healed.

He was the worst. You could always rely on him for that. But the old house does be quiet without him ...

Scab looked knackered lying by the hearth in the orange glow, like a faded bloodstain on the rug. Dead still, as the fire flickered down to coals.

I could always rely on the fire to bring me back to myself. Like the river, I could stare at it forever. I was them both once and will be again, I'd say.

The two of us were flaked. Or maybe Scab was playing it flaked because he was hardwired to follow in the footsteps of his flesh and blood? It was hard to say. I knew feigning – I had to feign plenty enough. I knew it to be a performance fuelled only by contempt, but with Scab ... I couldn't call it.

Yawning, I kept my eye on the box and had some more thoughts. To help wash away the heavy ones I'd had cycling home. After them nasty youths put me in an unnecessarily evil state of mind – I'd been soured by those weasels. Despite my best efforts, their poisonous smoke had coiled its way into my brain. Probably mine and Scab's both! Because if I was plotting his murder on the bike, Scab was no doubt plotting mine behind in the backpack. It stands to reason. We were one who had become two only about ten minutes before.

Scab protected me from their infection, as best it could. It went above and beyond the call of family duty. And now that the old man is gone, maybe having Scab around doesn't have to be a bad thing. The feel of it there, asleep by the hearth. Maybe cohabitation can be sweet if it's with your real flesh and blood?

That's when it hit me – the perfect olive branch.

'Sleep there on the floor by the hearth, Scab. I will figure it all out for us tomorrow.' I stared at it. Daring it to move.

Scab gave a small ripple around its edge to signify it heard.

Satisfied, I stretched my arms above my head and walked out of the sitting room smiling, even though the head was still pounding.

Out in the hallway, I slipped on my coat and hat and hobnail boots as quietly as I could, then snuck down the kitchen way and out the back door. I took the bike with me too, in case she was in need of another cycle before bed.

The river was asleep. Dead still. Like glassy stone. I splashed a finger in, the one with the most muck.

Her surface shimmered with a million secrets. I was her once and will be again.

I took off my old hobnail boots and removed my camo trousers. By the light of the moon and a few sodium ones across the bank, my left leg looked so blank now … Compared to Scab's old plot on the right, it just looked flat and featureless, like a blank canvas. It felt like a wasteground, with nothing doing on it. A neglected resource. The rest of my pale body was the same.

I bent over, as little as necessary, to scrape off the last hardened flakes of the tabloids. Small wads of purply-black mulch. Itchy, itchy skin, pluck, *sssss* … A spot of blood, yes. The winter's chill coming off the river brightened the tingle around Scab's former plot, which meant the pain would soon be drawing to its end. This time it wasn't resentment I got from the itch, but a kind of hope.

Next, I removed my hat and coat and stripped off the rest of my underclothes. I laid everything out by the riverbank, flat and neat in my human shape, so to anyone out walking late, it'd look like a man dissolved.

I got up on the bike and pedalled her, keeping the back nice and straight. She purred lightly going over roots and bits of aul' branch, until I clicked her up into the highest gear and hammered her up the bumpy path.

I was mad to get it over with and get home to show Scab how many grazes I ended up with from the collision.

And as I sped past the old elder trees, I couldn't help but snort out my nose thinking of the looks on the mechanics lads' faces, of total shock and bafflement, after they found my smashed-up bike sitting outside their garage the very next morning.

ALLEYWAY

Written in London ... I think

THERE'S BEEN PAID LEAVE and rumours of permanent redundancies as the needs of the Company evolve, but nothing is official. And the best way to stay prepared for eventually going back in and moving up floors is to keep up my journey into work in the morning.

MySchedule™ is everything. Margaret. She keeps me on the progress express.

I am a big believer in automation. Why do the opposite of maximising your creative and educative thinking time by trudging through swamps of admin? Get automation software to do all that for you. I read a quote online – 'Procrastination is just slow-moving failure.'

For example, MySchedule™ offers me lots of easy-to-absorb schedule templates, with names like Reflective and WorkHorse, depending on which option best characterises how I'm feeling at the start of that week. I can input all my online lectures, sync physical training programmes from other apps and add second and third language-learning sessions. I am learning Mandarin Chinese, because it's not just the *Economist*™ that's saying Mandarin is the new language of international business. Obvious huge asset to the Company. And also Esperanto, just in case I turn out to be right that in my lifetime the world finally comes to its senses, and we all unite under one language. English is the language of tourism. It's no longer about borders. Mandarin will conquer English, and all other languages, after it graduates fully to the language of wealth, money and power. I am acting now on an obvious future trend that everyone sees but just ignores. All the ostriches that don't mind the taste of sand. The ones who choose not to own up to themselves and admit that success takes hard work and innovation. The correct combination of the aforementioned will have landed me my first million by thirty-five, forty at the latest, I expect. Then from there the ascent is easy. Money makes money and I am thankful that I have been gifted all this free time.

Why waste valuable time doing anything that is the opposite of forwards?

MySchedule™ is my best friend. My shrink. My drill-sergeant. All in one easy-to-use app. In audio settings, I gave her the voice of Margaret Thatcher – that uptight, scary British vibe to make her the opposite of easy to disobey.

She gifts me access to distilled versions of hundreds of different personal growth training programmes, which I have the power to custom mix. Everything I need for mind, body and spirit, fitness, finance, she's got me covered. She boils it all down to something called the Success Circle.

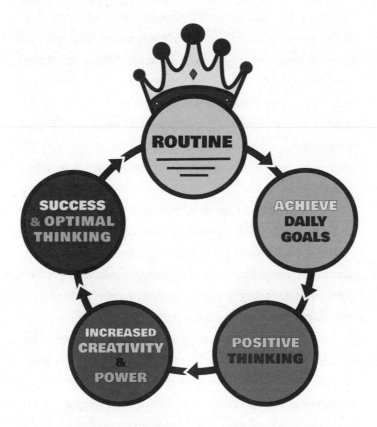

It's so simple – just apply the technique. Step by step. The Company will be left with no alternative but to find me another role. They'll be on their knees begging so that the competition loses out on the opportunity.

Margaret has been invaluable in keeping my life on track during the transition.

Good morning. Come along, wake up – it's 6 a.m. Bleep bleep, she calls out over the British army 'First Call' bugles. She is synced to my moving Mobi Alarm Clock™ which rolls around the room, hitting me from all sides. My housemate, Edwin, has threatened to make an official noise complaint, but that's only on the very rare morning when I sneak a Snooze behind Margaret's back.

6 a.m. Stretching and bodyweight exercises for thirty minutes. My bones creak and crack like crazy first thing! Like an old wardrobe.

6.30 a.m. Half-hour core-strength circuit workout with kettlebells.

7ish. A hot/cold shower. I read a science article on *Men's Iconic*™ mag online that said if you alternate from hot to cold, as extreme as you can go, you create growth hormones, super-hot shock proteins, which saves energy being wasted on repair and gifts me the best chance at maximising my day.

7.30 a.m. Having thoroughly shocked the body, then it's a thorough towelling. I use a stainless-steel window squeegee that I found in a teacher's backyard in college to wipe the mirror clear of steam. Clear mirror for full visibility as I ear-, nose- and brow-tweeze check. Brush and floss. Nail and pube check. I allot two good minutes for applying fungal jock-itch cream. Apply one of four or five different cold-pressed refined oils. It's good to keep them on rotation. Argan, olive, coconut, almond, and … Sugar, idiot – remember the other one. I need to relabel. They've gone all sodden and peeled.

I keep the oils in these cute little carry-on-luggage-friendly brown glass bottles I bought in a Marrakesh bazaar last year. They have red and golden tassels hanging off the lid. They fit so neatly in my toiletry travel case, but sadly most of the tassels have fallen off now. You get what you pay for. I will pop on the Post-it™ to-do list a note to remember to replace them with mason jars. Cool old ones with the branding in the glass. I wonder if they make them small enough to be carry-on-luggage friendly? I'd be appalled if they don't. When I'm rehired, I plan to celebrate by completing a Big Feel-Good Task. Maybe a week's vacation – Margaret can stay at home – to have fun, let the hair down, if it grows back! Somewhere warm with lots of local educational and historical attractions so I don't waste my entire time just getting drunk.

I shaved my head when my role was made redundant to optimise not having to shampoo and condition my hair. I need all the hours possible to keep pace and maximise adaptability. No hair means that once in a blue moon I can use that time to stay a little bit longer in bed – if I'm very sore from training or whatever.

8 a.m. (typically, hands-up truthfully here, I'm here by 8-ish, 8.30 at the very latest. I don't beat myself up for being a tad late – self-punishment leads to self-flagellation, which leads to the opposite of productivity.) Breakfast! Bon appetit. I chop fruit and hit Planner audio: *Your day ahead.*

Drumroll, Margaret. She reveals what tortures she's got planned!

If you achieve all tasks, you will earn one hundred and fifty points. I invite you to succeed!

She always invites me to succeed. Power smoothie with banana, maca and cacao, and shredded wheat with soy milk. The healthiest of all the cereals and it saves me so much time. It also buys me a cheeky Feel-Good Task later on in the park.

Then it's a quick five to ten to gauge the weather and pick out my outfit to fit the day. I allow myself no time to choose my clothes, like all the tech giants. Finally, I'm fully optimised for the outside world.

Every day on my commute, at exactly the halfway point to completing my journey, I pass this alleyway. Just beyond the busy cross-streets, officially inside the border of the Municipal Corporate District. And that's about Wrigley's Juicy Fruit™ time. I pop a stick in case I have to kiss anyone Paris-style twice on the cheek or whatever at work and don't want to be remembered by my rancid morning breath. I have never gone into the alleyway. I would rather hold it and pee at home. It is a stinky, drizzly slither of nothing between two places.

On an unlucky morning, I see this little thin man who lurks down there. All wrists. He is always the most awake person I see that hour. He has this electricity plaguing him. He wears old silver Christmas tinsel like a feather boa. He is always ranting and waving his arms and saying stuff like, 'No, no none of you, no, no none of you.'

Stamping in bare feet, the poor wretch. I saw him hunkered down once scratching and scratching at the ground. His feet and hands were bloody. Makes my teeth go on edge thinking about him.

Just as well it's Wrigley's Juicy Fruit™ time – time to chew quick and hurry. When Margaret catches me out dilly-dallying she throbs red at me. She hates wasted time. For every significant action of my day, she insists I explain myself. But chewing gum is the opposite of unproductive so I'm more than happy to credibly input:

Action – Chewing chewing gum.

Utility – Drowns out unwanted scratching noises and gives my jaw muscles a great workout.

Result? – Keeps me on task. Makes me more alpha.

Application of result – I appear in more favourable genetic health to my coworking friends.

Margaret throbs green.

Forty-five-minute walk to work – check.

My walk right now is not quite to work. It's to the park right next to work, along the east-side edge of the Corporate District. My building's entrance faces southeast. Only one way in or out for everyone still working on my floor: through the big glass front doors.

The park is perfect to input because it's practically the same distance from my house. Give or take a few hundred yards. The park is my new corner office. And the park is my new gym. Margaret revels in torturing me.

Only thirty more seconds: push it. Haaard.

She frogmarches me around that park with a sharpened stick, until I can barely keep my smoothie down, any chance she gets, which is … most days.

I've prepped my backpack the night before so I can create my mobile workstation.

Item Inventory:

Manduka Pro™ yoga mat – I went with the most hardcore.

iPad™ work tablet – I got a sweet deal with zero per cent finance at the checkout stage.

Mobile Belkin™ Pocket Power 5K battery – for extra juice.

Ideas notepad w/ bamboo pen – to chronicle any and all helpful visualisations.

Collapsible KeepKüp™.

Water bottle w/ powerful vacuum insulation, plus chopped lemons.

All housed in and on my sturdy Booq™ backpack. It's like a ninja back-shield.

Jersey and joggers in side-bag to complete physical training. I always train in bare feet. Even in the cold. It's good for the electrons.

Once my workstation is set up, I can complete my daily online coursework and language study. The park is also my very own university campus. Right now, I am absorbing a course entitled Soft Skill Development and Personality. Qualifications get you the job, but improving soft skills helps you retain it *and* climb the promotions ladder to reach greater heights. The pinnacle of supreme happiness. Soft skills mean appealing traits. Self-confidence, visionary thinking, social grace and effective communication.

Bargain, to think that I paid only a grand and a half for fifty lectures, each with their own individual headings. Lecture 1: Planning and Goals. Lecture 4: Understanding Human Perception and Personal Growth. Lecture 8: Interpersonal Conflicts. Lecture 15: Tone of Voice Is Everything! How to apply techniques to fully develop the tone of voice to positively influence others. Studies show it's not the words, it's the noises behind them.

The lectures are usually between one and two hours. Margaret challenges me to three lectures a day, broken up by my Duolingo™ Mandarin and Esperanto sessions. I am firing on all cylinders. I am already up to Lecture 4.

On my yoga mat, I always put the same tree between me and work. Better I'm not seen by anyone in the office right now as things shift around. Most of them don't know about my personal voyage of self-improvement. Only Derek the floor manager, to whom I send weekly updates. In the subject heading I was inspired to put 'Progress Express'.

But if you were the opposite of bothered, you wouldn't care about seeing who on your floor does and doesn't continue to have a job. I do not invite that kind of energy. I am too busy. I have too much to do. Drill-Sergeant Margaret keeps me fully focused on the task at hand. It doesn't matter who still does and does not have their jobs right this second. The needs of the Company rapidly evolve.

I decide I'm not exactly in WorkHorse mode, so I start off easy by switching my first lecture for a language game. It's a rockfall game on my tablet called *Debris*, where pieces of debris fall flying from a cliff face and my task is to catch them before they hit the street. I read on the Duolingo™ website that games are scientifically proven to teach you languages. Each piece of debris represents a word in Esperanto. When I catch one in mid-air it takes me to a multiple-choice question. After two hours, the best I do is six out of ten. Margaret's notifications are on. She bings and red badges to remind me that:

Every failure is tomorrow's challenge.

A spoon is not a full cutlery set but you have to start somewhere. Speaking of, nothing was ever achieved on this empty a stomach. So I take her advice and go get my lunch. A little early today, but I will make it up this afternoon by pounding all three lectures.

The Old Glover's Café where I get my lunch also fits perfectly. It's situated in the plaza beyond the park, right before you take a left and get to my office's front doors. They do vegetarian soup with sandwich and optional extra bread with butter for $7.95. Rustic vibe, with a wind-up gramophone cabinet but all the ceiling ventilation exposed like Starbucks™. I don't usually stay long, otherwise Margaret and I run the risk of bumping into someone who Derek didn't fire. I do not want that.

A little heavy on the spending for lunch, but it definitely qualifies as a Feel-Good Task. A treat I indulge in maybe one or two times a week or … cold hard truth version? On a rare occasion, four times. But very rare. *Debris* reminds me of this other app game where you're a ball rolling down a hill. It benefits my hand–eye coordination. As the game progresses, more difficult obstacles come up the hill. Bigger and bigger and bigger and some even jump and shift. And it is staggering the level of joy it gives me besting them all. Whoever thought to create that in virtual form definitely occupies space in the Success Circle. Or in one of the programmes from which it is derived.

Mrs Thatcher jolts me in my seat and throbs orange to notify me that it is 3 p.m. and I ought to go finish off the rest of the day's work. I decide today I am not returning to the park … I am returning to the gym. I will work out for one hour. Get my heart rate up, which will get my creative juices flowing. Boost my absorption. Healthy body, healthy mind. I think the Greeks said that.

The Old Glover's Cafe is right next to the store, and I high five myself when I remember to buy the Mars™ bar for a treat after I finish today so that I don't have to make another erroneous trip in the wrong direction later on the way home. A thought with real value, and the mind is such a powerful tool.

Walking home, eating my treat for later, I explain to myself why I did not complete any of my tasks. I harness the power and unknot the leaden feeling in the belly just by thinking. One of the golden rules is that everyone has the power to gain dominion over their thoughts, sensations and emotions. I am thankful for the Mars™ bar. *It is only because you hoped you would get more done, you hoped you'd be walking home with a sense of achievement in your stomach right now instead of an empty, heavy feeling.* That's OK too. Today's failure is tomorrow's challenge. It is only 4.45 p.m. – there is plenty of time in the rest of the day. Home, some squats. Which should warm me up into a full workout. I will feel great, I will be boosting my growth hormones which, on a biochemical level, is the same as reversing death. I ache in the shadow of that looming building anyway. Kudos to me for staying that long today as near as I did. I ate well. I got lots of fresh air. I learned Esperanto. I am developing. I am evolving. I am in the cocoon right now but nature doesn't let the butterfly stay in the cocoon. It's cyclical. Nature is a Success Circle. I just have to close the ring for there to be harmony. Just like salmon do when they lay their eggs, just like caterpillars do when they cocoon and become a butterfly. Why can't you close the ring? What's wrong with you?

Once I finish the Mars™ bar, I pledge to side run the rest of the way home. Once it settles.

The streetlight flickers on and makes the dread of winter stretch something thin inside. Such precious few hours of daylight we're getting these evenings. I take a headphone break because my ears hurt, and I hear this dry rustling. Like a tinsel monster. I didn't notice, but I am at the alleyway. My Samsung Galaxy S20™ screen throbs red. Margaret is cracking the whip – she definitely has a cruel streak.

That alleyway zombie is always wide awake first thing. He must've blacked out by now. I squint. The noise is coming from beyond the rim of the black shadow, where I can't see. It gets louder and more erratic. I activate Torch in my widgets to see what we're up against.

The alleyway man is there, by the yellow corner dumpster. Closer to me than I was expecting, so I hold my breath just in case. He is ignoring my Torch. He is clutching a huge dead Christmas tree. It's wrapped in red and gold tinsel. He is barefoot. His feet are blue from cold and black with dirt. He wears a long, black, very, very snug-fitting raincoat. It's way too small for him. He is taller than I gave him credit for. He is peeling off the Christmas tinsel and throwing it into the dumpster. He stamps softly. 'Used to be here ought to be that's what they want who took it away!' He does jerky pointing gestures down at his feet. His hands are wretchedly scabby and bloody. He hunkers down, scratching raw-fingered with his spine sticking out at me.

'Here! And they take it all away they take it all away angry they took no from you, all of us?'

His thin black hair is tied up in a haphazard bun. It sticks out the top of his head like a fountain. There's nobody else watching on the street. He gets a clutch-hold of the Christmas tree that's even taller than him. His spindly wrists poke out far too far. We suffer the bad luck to lock eyes, and the whites of his expand to even bigger bulbous bubbles.

Stamping. 'Relief relief. It used to be here! Up and down and no more nothin' no chance.'

He is peeling more layers of tinsel off the Christmas tree. He flails his arms over his head trying to get it in the dumpster. A big piece of gold tinsel goes around his collar and he just gives up and leaves it and sighs and moves on to the next piece. For the first time in as long a while as I can recall, I think, fuck it. 'You want a stick of gum?'

I slide out a Wrigley's Juicy Fruit™, away from its fellow silver-suits, and proffer it to him like a child feeding a cheetah a Chipstick™ through the bars of its cage.

'No don't eat poison, relief! First, they take it all away and then they hold you down by the shoulders and force feed you poison. To eat poison don't eat that. Plastic made from lunchbox. Lunchbox eat you with sugar will put you deep in your grave relief, don't eat that it poison.'

His whines are in such a whiny fox tone of voice that it screams self-abuse. He keeps tapping his blackened right heel. My face boils hot and red like I'm about to be killed. I feel stupid. I want to be at home in the shower covered in Radox™. Someone somewhere is filming on a faraway camera and Alleyway Man is just acting crazy and slapping at the ground to distract me and I'm about to get robbed.

He is propping himself against the dumpster and using the trunk to pound the ground.

'Take what away?' I say.

He lurches the tinselly tree forward and hammers the ground with the heel of his left hand. Lots of dried blood.

'What do you mean? What thing they have taken away from us? Call me crazy.'

'Crazy crazy crazy.'

I check behind me. Every move he makes feels like a decoy.

'Sod!' he shrieks. 'Softness and blades tickling that slink our toes …'

He tries to wipe away the ground like sand, like it wasn't there five minutes ago. Luckily, a technique I was inspired to absorb comes to mind; To win someone's full attention, go up and teach them something about themselves. But I can't think of anything for Alleyway Man.

'Hey, did you know that Joshua trees aren't trees? They're succulents.'

'… that comes up from the beyond the core in the bank account. They block the soul and give us our car ground, and lorries.'

Stamp. Stamp! It's not so much stamping, it's more shivering. Like somebody behind the dumpster has him plugged him into an electrical socket.

'Human feet meat! And he doesn't care he knows who his friends are.' He points up. I assume 'he' means the sky? 'He doesn't care. Or maybe, maybe he does care but how can he get access to the child. They can't talk because they poured this stuff everywhere and now he …' He drops the tree and is stamping around in a circle. 'Is … on … his own! Relief. And is lonely…'

He falls to his hunkers. 'He cries and gloomy. It's here it's there, there's no … Relief relief relief.'

He groans and staggers slowly to his feet. Stretches his wasted arms and his eyes and his head up to the sky. He looks like a Joshua tree. His face curdles up in a squint. And then he drops himself and limps slowly right past me, out of the alleyway onto the street. I've never seen him out this far. Nobody else is around. Everybody is at home watching television. He looks around, up and down and up in the sky.

He jumps in the air and brings his force down on the street like a polar bear. A car slows down and comes to a halt right in front of him. They gift him three or four seconds' grace, then start honking their horn. But not just honking – leaving the heel of their hand on the horn so it's a perpetual honk that makes your whole body shiver.

Alleyway Man hunches over, racked, with his eyes pinched shut and puts his hands over his ears.

A flash glimpse at my FitBit™ tells me that I'm actually ahead of schedule on my daily steps. Awesome! I slip off my sturdy Booq™ backpack to act as a shield in case he spits at me or something, and venture into the street to get him.

He is all gristly to the touch. The driver will not stop! I flash the 'cut it' sign, but it comes off more like a sieg heil, so cringe! Alleyway Man shrinks away from me. He rips off his tinsel scarf and throws it onto the guy's windshield. The driver door opens threateningly. Guy leans out of the car. Foreign-looking dude with a moustache, he looks like someone who wouldn't start anything. He throws a few hand gestures at me, urging us out of the way. I guide Alleyway Man off the street. He meticulously stomps and stamps every step, looking for a hole in the ice.

I say in my best nurse's voice, 'Let's go somewhere where there's grass. OK?' He won't budge. 'Come on, let's go to the park. It's not far. Feel the grass on our feet.'

But he's clearly not in the mood to help himself. He edges back up the alleyway, beyond the dark rim of shadow, and is gone.

What a poor, sad man. I visualise a big yellow Post-it™ and make a note to bring him some disinfectant the following morning. I scribble DETTOL™ in big capital letters.

Every failure is tomorrow's challenge. Margaret always knows what to say.

As soon as I get in the door, I indulge in a long, hot shower to wash the day off. A shower is a journey. It officially counts as a task. The quest to be clean! And as such, once I've vanquished that dragon I can reeeaally feel good. In the evenings, I only do hot. I do not do alternating hot and cold. I figure once a day is plenty. And what's the point in sparking yourself up just hours before bed? A shower cleanses and centres. Especially if I complement it after with some fizzy cucumber water. Makes it like I'm in a proper high-end luxury resort. It's the little touches.

7 p.m. (ish) – I lay sprawled, all pink, on my Simba Hybrid™ super-king mattress, swaddled in my favourite

bathrobe that I stole from Trump Plaza™ on my New York trip four years ago. Urgh, my stomach won't stop going on and on. I am being punished for eating that Mars™ bar too fast. These evenings are so dark. They go on forever.

OOOOWWW! Ugh. Enough already with the endless copulating in our backyard. Fox's tones of voice scream self-abasement.

In my bedroom, I am surrounded by what few sticks of furniture there are left. Most of my possessions and books and stuff are in little piles on the floor. The bailiffs even snatched the bedclothes – hilarious! But in a way, it's a gift. It means once I'm rehired, it will be such an easy moving day to my own bigger place. Because fuck Edwin and his constant moans and threats of noise complaints and his insistence that we use separate toilet rolls. And how he never has people over when I am around – I have proof. How I never once heard the words 'thank you' pass his lips, even after I did the place up to the nines. Flat screen, gold-leaf wallpaper, corner couch with built-in speakers.

But when those two fat, stinking bailiff losers took one look at my Simba Hybrid™ super-king they thought, *No way. Hernia!*

Our next-door neighbour is an even more tragic case. We can tell he's always finding excuses to escape to the toolshed to hump his Bosch™ *yakka-dakka-dakka* jackhammer on the weekends and wake up the whole damn estate. Bosch™ are clearly a company who do an impressive amount of market research.

They know exactly the kind of men to target. Men like my neighbour, beyond their youth, who have given away most, if not all, of their power. But still want to feel powerful, still want to feel useful. Everyone wants to feel useful.

The *yakka-dakka-dakka* noise is the usual signal to get out the bunting and the booze because the weekend has begun. Every Saturday morning – he's the bane of our lives. Edwin and I have shared a chuckle over cereal about how this guy's marriage must be in a real state that he'd rather spend his weekends with a jack-hammer than with his wife, but we argued later about which one of us made the comment first.

OOOOWWW! Since I'm reminded of nature, I flick on my tablet and plant some trees in the Amazon. As many as I can afford. Right now, Margaret has my purse strings pulled tight. Planted! That officially counts as a task. *Congratulations, Nature's Hero!* The email pings through. Logged under category: Positive Acts. Margaret's screen throbs green. If the Feel-Good Tasks part of the programme breaks down, who knows what else could follow. I check on the status of a koala with third-degree burns that I adopted – *OOWWWWW!* All good – the koala is still alive.

Despite having washed off the day, my thoughts won't stop rabbiting on about Alleyway Man. The trees on *our* street seem fine. His Christmas tree was definitely dead but that one was not connected to the ground.

I have no more lightbulbs left. The lightbulb in my bedroom-ceiling fixture was the last one. Now they're all gone. I could steal one of Edwin's from his room because I know where they are, but I won't because all hell would break loose. I didn't factor lightbulb costs into my carefully designed MySchedule™ Money Planner. Now I'm going to have to review my whole outgoings. Or just do without lightbulbs …

My heart is trying to leap out of my chest. And I've got an irritating erection building. I should have had a wank in the shower – there's an opportunity to optimise. Make a visual Post-It™ note for next shower: Come, so I don't have to later wipe it off with tissue that I don't have. But I hate how it catches going down the drain.

Jacking off might calm me. No – positive visualisation, rechannel that energy. Use your mantra that you gifted yourself in secret. Onayot. Onayot. Onayot. Onayot. Onayot. Onayot. Onayot. Which, in secret, means innovation.

Men's Iconic™ says that innovation is a process that gives birth to itself. Which in turn gives birth to endless good ideas. Innovation is at the heart of all success. And gratitude is innovation's gas refill station. That's good. Did I read that in *The Success Circle*? If not, then I just came up with it. Better make a note of it just in case.

OK, close your eyes, breathe and find your centre. At your centre you will find your gratitude, the birthplace of all revelation. To materialise, you are floating weightlessly above a vast, silent highway. Like one from the old movies. Old future movies. The highway is fully lit like an electrical artery, but with no cars. It just stretches on forever – *OOWWWW!* – there are no trees, just highway. The landscape is flat and you thought you'd washed the day fully off but Alleyway Man is limping down the highway now. He's fleeing from … something invisible. He can barely stamp his feet any more – he's broken all the bones. He looks scared. He collapses in a heap. He is lying flat on the concrete. He jibbers like a wretch. He is crawling now with clenched fists. His black raincoat is in tatters and scrapes along the concrete, and his wounds are gaping and bleeding and he racks and fits on the ground.

Suddenly, I am hijacked by the memory of last week when I woke up with my arm sieg heiling under the pillow and how it made me feel guilty for the rest of the day.

But *I* scraped that gristly long mess off the street. *I* saved his life! I deserve to add that into Positive Acts. I wonder what happens to Margaret when I input that I saved a person's life? She must throb a whole different colour. Maybe golden?

OOOWWWW!

Today's failure … Today's failure … Today's failure …

I check MySchedule™. I now have exactly seven and a half hours before I have to be up and fully ready to honour the morning routine. My Fitbit™ is sporting a big green thumbs-up thumbnail with the racing-stripes smiley face which indicates that I've more than achieved my goal today. Anything else I do now would be a bonus.

I leap off my mattress. I drop my bathrobe to the floor and put on my roughest, toughest pair of jeans. I

215

slide my Friesian festival rainboots on. Margaret can come, but I'm turning off her notifications.

I tiptoe downstairs and into the kitchen so Edwin doesn't hear. I sneak a couple of plastic bags out of the plastic-bag drawer and tie them over my rainboots with elastic bands because, after a little eBay™ research, they should increase in value in three to four years once they've graduated to vintage status.

Edwin has this mask sitting on the kitchen shelf that he got at his office's Halloween party, with a freckly nose and gap-tooth grin from that 'funny' magazine *Mad*™. I pack that in my canvas tote bag.

Out into our backyard and that asshole sensor light comes on and sends my heart into my throat. I clear our back-garden wall like a shinobi into next-door's garden – ouch! – and make a beeline for their tool-shed. Their golden retriever knows me. He loves me. He's harmless. He wakes up in his too-small bed and flaps around and decides to follow me with his favourite toy in his mouth down the garden. What a thrill! It's always so fun to work a break in your routine into your routine.

The window of the neighbour's tool-shed is made from blue tarp lazily stapled down. I activate Torch in my widgets, stick my hand through and easily unlatch the door from the inside. Edwin was clearly wrong. This guy can't care that much about his beloved yakka-da-kka-dakka, otherwise he'd have embedded it behind much tighter security.

Inside the tool-shed, I find her standing in an old oil barrel, encrusted with concrete chips. The

BOSCH BRUTE 27 VC 100V™ cordless jackhammer. Maximum power. Low vibration. ID'd on the online catalogue from my bedroom window weeks ago.

I hold position in the quiet for a second and admire her. I anoint her with the name of Jackie. A little obvious but, hey, I read somewhere that to possess a machine and not give her a name is bad luck. And the last thing I need is more bad luck. Jackie means Business – she looks so cool. She looks like a folded-up stormtrooper. I shine the light on Jackie's side. I easily find her On switch on the handlebar. Middle-aged-idiot-proof. Damn thing is heavier than I thought, though, so I haul her into his wheelbarrow.

In chapter twelve of the book, *The Success Circle* teaches that it's not the task itself but preparation for the task that yields worthy results. And making lists is a strong part of my game.

Jackhammer: Check.
Sledgehammer: Check.
Body-length crowbar: Check.
Predator Lightning™ Welding Gauntlets: Check.
Face protector: Check.

I whip on my *Mad*™ face protector. Better to mask up now before I show up – there are probably a million street cameras. I lug all the stuff in his wheelbarrow up the side passage of his house. My plastic-bag boots are so noisy, I hope him and his wife take medication. On top of everything else, I do not need to be slapped with

a burglary charge. Plus, I'm not stealing anything. I'm
just borrowing Jackie. He'll never have to know, and
even if he does find out he should be proud that she
was put to some real use.

My golden retriever pal flaps around and jumps up
on the barrow.

'G'boy. Down!'

I roll Jackie out of their driveway quick and onto
the quiet street. Our estate is called Ocean Beach even
though it's sixty-two miles from the coast on GPS. What.
A. Thrill. I feel fifteen again, stealing mobile traffic
lights! I step her up to a swift jog and Jackie's hammer
rattles in the barrow. By my guesstimation, running her
at this speed should cut the journey in half.

I am clicking my heels with the thrill of knowing
that I'll have so many extra steps done for tomorrow
morning. I'm on track to reach the second tier of my
Fitbit™ daily record. Margaret is synced up; she will
not be capable of disguising the surprise in her voice!

I get to his alleyway and toggle my stopwatch. Eleven
point four minutes – not bad, but I forgot the Dettol™
disinfectant – fuck! Visualise each phase properly and
completely, you total idiot, duh. Why can't you learn?

The night is icy still. The streets are empty. Nobody
lives in the Municipal Corporate District.

I activate Torch and creep out of the streetlight, into
the dark rim of shadow. I feel a shortness of breath. The
hairs are standing up on the back of my neck. I am a
million per cent sure Alleyway Man is crouched and
poised, ready to lurch at me and clamp his wretched

diseased hands around my throat. A faint rustling comes from the dumpster.

Alleyway Man is sleeping, three or four Christmas trees deep. They rise as he breathes like a hedgehog. It's the stillest I've ever seen him be. I wonder how many hours he sleeps. I'd guess only two or three. I wish I could take a leaf out of his book. He jiggers a little under the dead trees like a dog chasing a cat, except his dream is definitely less fun.

I get Jackie in position, while trying to breathe the shaking out of my hands. I am a rock. I'm that big sacred red boulder that my cousin was waving from the top of on Instagram™ in the Outback. My palms are sweating.

Leaning my upper bodyweight onto Jackie, I grip firm and flip her to On. *YYYAKKA-DAKKA-DAKKA-DAKKA-DAKKA!* She *drenches* the alleyway in noise!

She's so loud, I can't hear above the ringing tone in my ears. *YYAKKA-DAKKA-DAKKA-DAKKA!*

I face toward the yellow dumpster in case he thinks I'm some kind of villain because of the *Mad*™ mask and lunges at my throat with his scabby hands. Also, I want to catch him waking up. I am so looking forward to Alleyway Man's Total Makeover™ moment, but even with Jackie bouncing off the walls, the Christmas trees don't budge.

In a rare moment, I am powerless to stop a terrible negative visualisation bubbling up. This time, it's Jackie shattering both my eardrums like popcorn kernels. Stupid idiot, you should've borrowed the neighbour's ear protectors too. I am rapidly ageing my hearing capacity here now, but then, eureka, I'm gifted another revelation. From the bottom of my canvas tote I pull an ancient flat pack of Kleenex™. I spit on them and stuff both ears so Jackie and I can continue yakka-dakka-dancing.

I can just about hear my breath hissing inside Edwin's mask. Thank goodness it's plastic because otherwise there would be no Odor-Eaters™ on earth strong enough get my sweat stink out.

The ground pulses and shatters into lumps. It comes away just like Styrofoam™. So satisfying! Like the crunchy golden happy bit inside the Butterfinger™. I always loved the Butterfinger™. You could nibble off the chocolate layer and then it feels like you're holding a trophy.

Another annoying visualisation bubbles up and catches me off guard. This time of Jackie jolting out of my grip and yakka-dakka-ing straight through my foot. But using a technique I mastered, I convert the image into a higher focus. I feel so grateful to myself for having the foresight to steal Edwin's mask. Not only to hide from all the CCTV cameras, but also to protect my face from all the kicked-up dust and shards. My mind takes credit that that was the idea all along, even though I know better.

Jackie is so deafening. I don't have that much time, and *still* not a peep from the dumpster.

I double-laser-focus down to hammer out a perfect square. The ground shatters and flakes to dust. We make a great team, Jackie and I. We are Power at achieving tasks. If only I was gifted this kind of support at work, instead of constant comments and disciplinary sessions, I'd be unstoppable.

Make a visual Post-it™ note to self to later jot down in Ideas notepad: Research jobs in demolition while work restructures! That would generate some serious electricity. I could pawn back some of my stuff. It would get my steps through the roof, improve definition in my upper body. Improve my sleep. So exciting. Margaret will be so pleased.

I'm awarded my second Fuck It moment of the day, and decide to widen the perimeter into a rectangle. Just imagine if I had Jackie every day at work. You can't fake this kind of Power. To think, I gave so many years of my life to them. My best years, my most useful years, when I was at my brightest and most energetic, and they rip it all away and give me what in return? Nothing. Nothing nothing nothing! Just a fuck-you goodbye? Well, FUCK YOU GOODBYE COMPANY!

Double double fuck it, because Jackie and I have the Power to go as far as we like. We shatter on down as far as where he stamped out onto the street today. I'm constructing him a nice little run.

Turns out I was wrong. There are a *lot* of people who live in the Corporate District! They cluster over on the far side of the street. If only they could see my big coat-hanger grin, wider than the one on the mask – ha! Some of them are laughing like they're happy, like me.

YAKKA-DAKKA-DAKKA! Most of them look very angry, throwing their arms up in the air and looking up the street, hoping someone will come and help them. Poor sheep.

Some are filming. I must make quite a sight. I must look like a supervillain! A shaved-head guy in a *Mad*™ mask jackhammering in the middle of the night. This is viral gold. Trust my luck that I'd go viral with a mask on. Post-it™ note visual: Google 'Masked alleyway jackhammer man' every day for the next week during stretches to see if anything comes up.

Oops! Another visual bubbles, this time of Edwin: arrested and charged. Cuffed and taken out of the house. Framed for destruction of property. I am peering out from behind the curtains of my bedroom window watching. The beer-bellied neighbour stands by his gate with his arms crossed, next to his scowling wife in a pink bathrobe with curlers in. Edwin is shouting, 'It wasn't me, it wasn't me!' If that happened, I'd probably let it play. I'm not going to throw myself on the train tracks.

The future always begins as an idea. And we all have the power to summon the future so, in a way, that's now happened to Edwin.

The bare-earth run is now pretty fully shattered – high-five. High-five myself again because he *still* hasn't woken up! The shattered run is kind of crooked, like a fat, rusty scimitar.

I pull up all the bigger pieces and sling them behind the dumpster – making sure to only bend from the waist, keeping my core engaged. I am making Margaret award me at least a hundred Fitness Points for all this.

There could be anything beneath these slabs! Human bones, treasure, ancient aliens or clay pots and sticks of people's furniture from ten thousand years ago. Portals to lives long past. I wonder did they have bailiffs back then too? We are unlocking so much Power here. The Power of the Past – oh my god, I should write that book! But start it as a blog, so it's less pressure.

I get low to whistle at the bare earth, but I don't know any tunes off by heart so I just whistle one note – *WHEEEEEEEEEEEEEEEEE!* – to wake up all the plants. As I whistle, I scratch at the topsoil – it's rock hard.

It's only after I've switched Jackie to Off that the Christmas trees finally twitch.

I wriggle out of my plastic-covered rainboots and socks quick. He climbs very slowly out of the dumpster. His body is older than his years. I help him down the other side. His trousers are rags. His feet touch the bare earth. My eyes are to his chin. He slowly spreads his fingers wide like fans, then stretches them above his head. He was definitely a Joshua tree in a past life. He squints his bulging eyes and stamps lightly. He digs his heels in. He treads slowly down our new run. His steps are careful and completely silent. He's like tall Ghandi. Kicking bits of debris off the newly bared earth, he strolls around our new garden with the streetlights behind him.

I am huffing behind the mask in efforts to return myself to homeostasis, twelve breaths per minute, when he wanders up to me. 'Grass-bringer core direct. Earthen friend.'

Softly, he touches my plastic nose. Up close his eyes are scarred with veins like he spent too much time upset and the wind changed. He looks down at her by my side.

'Jackie', I say. 'Her name is Jackie.'

He gazes at her for a long time. He places a filthy long hand on her gleaming white veneer. He bares his three teeth to the three stars in the sky. 'Bubbling up between our toes HA HAAAA crazy. Well done you, Crazy.' He does a laugh made of short intakes of breath.

Yet *another* Positive Act springs to mind. If I don't slow down at this rate I'll be canonised. 'Here, you take Jackie. *Shhh.*' I make a shushing motion on my mask lips. 'Crazy will bring you grass and things to grow.'

He lifts Jackie up to hugging height, oddly without much difficulty. He whispers something to her. I know he won't risk losing her by using her. A looooong breath hisses from his nose, like she responded. Jackie and Alleyway Man disappear back into the dumpster. A king and queen retiring to their royal bed.

I am so sweaty and clammy and red-faced but who cares! I take a big bow, which delivers me a double-pronged benefit. First prong is it gives the phone pointers a great cutting point. Second prong is it gives me a much-needed whoosh of air under my *Mad*™ mask.

I'm glad the show's over now. I didn't realise how looking forward to being alone I was.

My feet revel in my work. My toes tickle the topsoil for a while. Until they go freezing and I can't stand it any longer. Hunkered down, I whistle whatever notes come to mouth and scrape chunks of flattened soil into my fists to get a direct line on the earth's core. Like Crazy's friend Alleyway says, ha. Hysterical!

Walking home alone, and that is the longest I have gone in a *long* time without thinking about work. Without thinking about the Company. Wow ...

I feel elated. My feet won't stay on the ground! Thrilled and humbled to be the honoured recipient of Alleyway Man's revelation.

Of a whole new world. No, a new old world. He will return things to the balanced way they *should* be. Bring this whole stupid charade crashing to the ground, because we're all just slaves, aren't we? Kept busy building something that's making us all more miserable.

He lives in a dumpster but his vision is far larger than any cheating Company's.

I'm buying another Jackie, I don't care. There must be a website where they do zero per cent at checkout. There will be, simply because I am determined to find it. And my determination times his innovation means we can achieve anything.

I'll come back tomorrow to hear more, but when *I* want to. Not when Margaret expects.

Also, do *not* forget Dettol™ disinfectant this time, duh. Idiot.

VENDING MACHINE

Written in Bali

IN MY MIND ... Ouch! Fucking nerve. Truck just made the thousand-mile mark and no pussy, just Highway. DEFCON 3. My balls are officially touching the floor of the cab. Launching Operation Good Feeling, Warm Feeling, here we go – In my Mmmmmmmm mmmmmmmmmmmmmmmmmmmmmmmmmmmind ... Take a prayer bead's worth of breaths, like in the singing bowl videos on YouTube. Relax fully, feel it in the gut from your head to your toes. Keep the windpipe open when back-of-throat humming, 'cos otherwise my teeth rattle. Teeth? Who's lying, Frank? Dentures. And remember, don't forget ... Mmmmmmmmmmm, now deepen the pitch of the Mmmmmmmmm, so the Mmmmmm goes right down, like cum down a beaver's neckhole.

God I'm thirsty. But I just passed the pickle park on the highway and there ain't another one for miles. And it's not like I'm in a position to wander very far from the rig and expect to keep my job. Piece of shit LoJack. The cops only got, like, ten per cent of their cruisers fitted with short range LoJack systems, and they've got to be in range of the signal? That's what passes for law enforcement these days. A game of hot and cold. Call me crazy but that doesn't exactly instil me with faith. Another driver working a bar-stool in Flagstaff told me that any thief with half a brain can go to Radio Shack, and for twenty bucks' worth of parts, build a contraption that broadcasts a ton of noisy frequencies to beat the onboard LoJack. Easy. And this guy was not the sharpest tool in the shed. So, if the rig ever gets jacked, it'll be pure dumb luck if it's found.

Ouch. C'mon remember, Frank. Deploy the positive memory technique – remember, like sitting on the banks of the Musselshell. That's always a good one. After that eternal ice finally thaws, that is – God that river could swell to a real huge size. Man, how the winters never let up, mmmmmmmmmm, forget about the winters, Frank. Endless asshole Montana … Life in the fridge. Getting up in May like it's still fuckin' Christmas. No wonder running truck seemed appealing after the army. Get to travel, get to see more of the country.

'If you're willing to work and willing to move, there's a job in Montana waiting for you!' Well, show me where to sign, Frank G. Wabash, there you go. That idiot with the haircut and the suit with the business card should never have been allowed anywhere near a US Army base. Bullshit – life sentence more like. You get to see highway and lots of it. And the more highway, the more highway. And the snowy wastes! And the endless shale fields, and the depressed oil assholes drinking coffee. Trashing pickle parks. Coffee with fuckin' syrup – animals. Stop it! Positive visualisation, Frank, positive, not fucking ...

In my mind, where I really am ... I ammmm, grinning like I own the place. I'm holding a glass of champagne, rolling a seven in a Monte Carlo casino. That's more like it. Wearing a white tuxedo like Robert Redford wore in that movie about cuckolding. I tried to stay awake to the part where he fucks that delicious Italian-looking gal, Demi Moore, and Woody Harrelson is really angry about it, but I fell asleep, and woke up later with a burned-out cigarette in the holder and no motivation to jerk off. I had to be back on the road in two hours and couldn't shake the dick nerve, and the guy in the next cab was heaving up his guts all night. So, I got a cup of coffee. Funny, when you're that turned around, it's like I'm not me. Like I'm tired but way more awake. I'm not-too-distant-future me, the me of the near future, who ain't up yet but who's gotta be up, driving. Diligent employee. Holding down the load, or floating above the dash on his jerry-rig, jerking it to naughty movies where the wheel ain't digging him in the side. But no more, sir, no more of that for me – it's a waste. It dulls the sword's edge. Gotta keep it sharp. We are well past a thousand ...

In my mind … Ow … I'm kind of thirsty. I'mmmm between the big thighs of a gifted brown woman called Kendra, or Divine, or Mangia. Man, I once saw this girl, only in a picture. She looked Italian, like Demi. She had 'Mangia' tattooed in italic letters up the inside of her thigh. I didn't know what it meant so I looked it up later after I hoisted up the gurney. And it's Italian for 'Eat'. By God, when that loaded up on Google Translate, it didn't take me twenty-five seconds. The guy in the next cab over must've thought I was having a panic attack! Those jerks were one in a million …

Yeah, Mangia, baby. And sure, I like the relaxation videos. They're nice to drive to and listen. According to a lot of traffic, some of the sonic frequencies of vibration do damage repair. It helps get under the hood, helps me relax, and it greatly mellows the dick nerve. But I am not one of those waifs who goes all Canadian about it. Or one of those idiots who ends up with the Coca-Cola plastered in Sanskrit across his beer gut.

Mangia. And it wasn't no tramp stamp – it was in beautiful italic lettering down the inside of her leg. In my mind, sadly only in my mind, I'm …

Ouch. Goddamn tail lift was broken and I was late and, sure, a little hungover – what ape isn't. I was strapped and had to make deliveries pronto. So I tried to gung-ho some barrels quick with some canvas straps, and fucked my crotch. Sitting in the cab all day and night doesn't make it better, but still it ain't the worst. Some guys haul truck for eight, nine, ten weeks at a time. Some can switch their brain off easy and some

guys can switch their dick off easy. Me, it works out I
need a beaver. Every thousand miles or so. Get loaded,
get a beaver, maybe two, depending on … A thousand
miles and after that I go down. Like clockwork. I start to
spin. It gets empty when it feels this full. And a decent
working-girl's body is like a poem after a thousand. Like
birdsong. And her pussy is the 'HOO-AHHH, passport
to heaven!', like Pacino says in that awesome movie
where he played the blind colonel. Oo-raa.

Man, the farmers out in these parts? Land around
here used to be worth five hundred dollars an acre and
now it's two hundred and fifty thousand. You don't got
to strike oil to strike oil …

Ouch, when the nerve catches like this, I found this
great video on YouTube that showed me how to relieve
it by rotating my leg around in its hip joint. I got all
kinds of positive visualisation playlists. Light reps, relaxation videos, all different-sized Tibetan singing bowls.

And why should I have to explain myself or be
embarrassed to say I'm on a voyage of self-improvement? What, the only voyage a man in this line of work
can be on is for the company? Most of these animals.
Some of us are making a little extra effort to grow, and
like it says in the videos, the emptier it is in there, the
cleaner. Noble silence. 'Cos I'm sick of the same old
carousel at the parks with these slobs overweight and
miserable, talking trash about everyone and leaving
passive-aggressive notes in the showers and everything
– they're a fucking poison. And on the carousel, and
around I go again and, in my mind …

I'm getting right up behind one of these toxic assholes and I'm driving a broken Coke bottle into his jugular. Putting him and his boxer shorts swiftly out of their misery. All the other gators scatter back to their cabs. The Coke fizzing against his gurgling. He lays there like a pale figurine, belly-up in a rest-stop parking lot, as I drive away knowing I just scored a point for Mother Nature. And even though that makes me real calm to think about, it only hurts me in the long run, according to YouTube. Nothing is better, apparently. Nothing at all.

But the videos do have the power to take your mind off those kinds of things. Off the carousel, and away from coming around to come face to face with the nozzle of my M4, sliding between the clenched teeth of the enemy. And sure, they made us all out to be dedicated and loyal and all that, but you put a gun in a man's hand, no matter who, you'll be damned if it doesn't compel him to examine the nature of things. The fear in another man's eyes. 'Innocent, innocent!' My ass.

But in my mind, come on, Frank … Launch Operation Warm Feeling already. I'mmmmmmmmmm, down on the banks of the Musselshell. That's always a strong one. It's warm and sunny. I must be only, what? Six years old? The birds are all woken up and hollering. She's sitting in the shade, trying to make the accordion play. But I'm just running around. Looking at butterflies and splashing minnows. I'm goading Bertha into the river. All the while she's just sitting there, trying to get a tune out of that damn thing in the shade of the tree, her yellow-and-white dress piled out all sides. Damned if that stupid whiny thing don't scare away all the animals, though! And I'm terrified, down by that riverside, to put those raggedy sneakers back on. I never thought to stuff them with my socks so some poisonous little asshole couldn't climb in there to wait for my toes. I make her get out of the car and check again, and she rolls her eyes all dramatic. She says those kinds of guys only exist around here in my library books, and that I have an overactive imagination, and that she would apple my cheeks.

She never needed to blab on and on to tell you a lot – we could always talk just in the way she touched my skin.

I met one girl a while back, Irene, who was between jobs but had a diploma in landscaping. Nice lady, cute little seat cover, but couldn't drive for shit. She nearly blew my door off on the highway, then she pulls up next to me at the traffic lights, all cool, in a cute little sky-blue convertible four-wheeler (her ex-husband's). I give her the trucker salute and a smile and she leans over like we always knew each other and says, 'You like McDonald's? There's one at the next rest stop.' Next thing you know, we got the drapes pulled and we're fucking in my cab and I came like a champ. And it was great, until it wasn't. I kick myself – the warning signs were all there. When her work dried, 'cos it turns out the oilers around Bell Creek don't give a shoot about having manicured lawns, she ups the drinking. I told her alcohol only makes your problems worse, but it was all, 'You knuckle-dragger this, piece of fat shit that, I don't need you! Who needs a man, especially one as ugly and as pockmarked as you.'

Then she'd say sorry and we'd make up, and we'd fuck like March hares. One night, she was so hot I left the house and went to sleep in my cab. She hated when I needed to get away – it just wouldn't do. So first, she kills my tarantula Brutus, who I entrusted her with. Then I wake up with her hovering over me in the cab, brandishing the bread knife with blood in her eyes. I could see the flames. She was going to murder me in my sleep. That was it. Now, once in a while, I see her little blue open-top parked at that rest stop. Trap primed and ready. Waiting on another guy's unsuspecting toes. I never stop there, not any more. Women are best off in pictures and videos – the real ones got too many booby traps. I miss her sometimes, though. You see, it's the good memories, the Operation Warm Feelings. They churn you in the gut and give you the temporary amnesia … They're the biggest booby trap of all. Get a beaver done instead, maybe two if you're feeling reckless. Every thousand or so.

In the mind … I can't even remember the last time I for real stopped and faced the sun; he and me definitely ain't friends. I used to draw him with cool sunglasses like Jimmy Dean and a big shit-eating grin. Rebel without a cause, not a care in the whole universe. I wish he'd show himself right now – come on, Jimmy. Let's stage a takeover! Some kind of big coup. A swift, militant usurpation. Oo-raa! I wish there was a civil war. I wish there was a big happy genocide or something, least there'd be something goin' on, at least it would be exciting for all of us, at least it would make a change – no, stop! Stop putting poison in your own tank, Frank.

I need a breather. Splash some water on my face. Hooooo. Stretch the legs. And I'm thirsty. Plus it's 1.45 in the a.m., and that's about prime beaver happy hour. They're always so pale because they're nocturnal. Most of the time you can't be sure she's healthy until you hear the tone in her voice. The sass always puts my doubt to bed ... And I really ain't had a piece since Bismarck? That's eleven hundred miles, if it's a day.

This park's usually quiet but, hey, we'll see. Cross fingers and toes. There could be one roaming around, building a dam near the payphones.

I step out of the cab. Stretch my arms and my neck, and take a cold breath. Beyond the perimeter of the lot, the snow-covered trees get pretty thick. If the sun rose behind them now I'd drink it like a cold beer.

On the double to get the blood moving and I drop my keys, and that old dick nerve thinks he has me beat, but he doesn't. I'm just observing its pain, not experiencing it. Observing it, not suffering it. Ssss, fuck it, but it does hurt though.

And why is it that the vending machines only ever sell shitty, addictive fizzy crap that turns kids fat before they've even got a chance, and puts you in your grave ten years premature?

And my keys are damp in my pocket. I'd prefer to hydrate with water or a fruit smoothie or somethin', and I'd part with a little more for the convenience. Occasionally, not all the time, because the healthy stuff is pricey. But you get the warm glow of satisfaction that goes along with it, which lasts for, what? At least a few hours, but then you need another top-up … Oh, fuck it, I'll get a Coke. It'll keep me, ouch, hammered down the rest of the way.

Fumbling under my keys for change, at the vending … machine … HMUHMUHMUHMUH-MUHMUHMUHMMMM – sound … Closes my eyes. Loosens my grip around the wet keys. Cold air goes in …

Way in. It fills me up.

UHMUHMUHMUHMUHMUHMUHMMMM, my body pulls in the deepest breath it's taken since I came out of my mother.

UHMUHMUHMUHMUHMUHMUHMMMM … It's … from the machine. A sonic vibration. Low. With this … needly pitch above, like kind of complementary.

Like two singing bowls. Now I'm taking a knee. Giggling! I'm tickled, from up my right arm into my body from the change hiding beneath the wet keys in my pocket.

The ground fizzes up on my knees like pop rocks.

UHMUHMUHMUHMUHMUHMMMM –

Dissolving the pain dissolving into the change into the keys dissolving into me HMUHMUHMUHMUH-MUHMUHMUHMMMM – ZZZZZZZZZZ –

Fallen. Knees? Feeling? Now? Nothing. Nothing at all. In particular.

Everything's ... vibrating. The pain around.

From the same source behind enemy line, where aware meets image. Inside the machine, vending the carousel around converting ... Everything.

To the same ... Radio frequency.

UHMUHMUHMUHMUHMUHMMMM –

That moment. Left nothing, nothing at all.

That moment. Nothing. The one just before ... When the vending machine changed everything into everything else.

Nothing more than ... Just that moment before ... The falling. When there was need ... to fall further into the fall. To make it fully sweet.

The ground crackles reward dissolving knees into ... Pop rocks. Ha, funny.

MUHMUHMUHMUHMUHMUHMUHMMM –

At a depth, below the surface of these little jazzy notes ... Crackling at a pitch that whisks us all back to an unknown century – Duh duh, duh dah, dah duh, duh dum, revealing ...

That moment.

As I fell to my knees, then I saw it – the whole carousel.

What's coming to face and what's moving away.

To a faraway view onboard the Dwight D. Eisenhower Highway, across the railroad causeway of my frozen Great Salt Lake, past my Rocky Mountains and off Grand Junction Highway 70 to my Monument Valley Highway 20 – and the whole way through to my Yellowstone Park.

My heart. Backs the carousel in a grace of harmonies, serenading the sun.

MHUMMHUMUHMUHM –

Thirsty, how my knees feel soaked, that could be blood, but … to hear that smile in their tune? And that they echo on for an age after the explosion of the sun?

And in that huge flash, none of them notice me, thawing … MHUMMHUMUHMUHM duh dum, dum dah, dah dum. Melting. Out where the winter water stops flowing. And shrinks my life to a passing whisper.

And sometimes there's shadow, and other times the rocks are splitting the sun.

And sometimes she's sitting there under the tree.

Fiddling with the keys of the old accordion. Her snap to hold its bellows closed, in extreme close-up, is hanging on by a thread. And sometimes she isn't there ... Which follows she always is. Making sound that grows the boughs of the tree stronger. From underneath. For our own everlasting shade ... is where I'm due to stay. To rejoin the lights of her flickering prayer. And hear my life as a passing whisper.

As it fades to the colour of snow ... Lightening ... Heightening ... Enlightening, enlighteniiiing ...

When from above, I get a shove. Somebody is poking me hard on the shoulder. 'C'mon, get up! If you –' MMHUMMMMHUMMHMMHUM '– to buy something, you'll have to vacate the lot. What are you –' MMHUMMMM '–eed medical attention?'

My neck snaps up and my hands are splayed out in front, laying in the cold ice sludge, in what's known on YouTube as 'child's pose'. They're all blue, like a corpse. Ouch.

Another shove. If he hits me with one more jab in the shoulder ... 'Oh, thank God, he's moving. Come on, pal, naptime's over.'

I try and get up. Get to my feet on the double.

The vending machine throbs bright white and red. With a Coke bottle on the front, glistening with condensation, being held up to the open mouth of a full-lipped brunette. Her eyes are pinched closed in rapture. Above her it says, 'Always the real thing'.

I hear the guy scurry away on the phone to the maintenance company, saying, 'We got a problem with this machine. Yeah, I think it's broken …'

I stamp around in circles to get the blood moving and clap the terrible chill out of my hands. Crack, crick, crick, crack, groan, cough. And the only heat I feel is from the eyes of two gators inside by the coffee station. Yeah, drink your coffee, assholes. Nothing to see here.

I catch the manager's eye, still talking on the phone. What's the matter, champ? Never seen a guy worship a vending machine before? I'm so desperate for a Coke, but I can't feel my fingers to put in the change. And I am not walking past those assholes inside the store, giving them the satisfaction.

The sky is going pale grey. No Jimmy Dean this morning. Dammit, that means I'm late. I better haul ass. I haven't put in a notify, and work will be calling if I don't show up. How long was I –? Ouch.

Better get the hammer down so I can avoid the brake check. Then, I'll curtain the cab and hoist the jerry-rig, just for an hour or two. Hope to god I can jerk myself to sleep. Mangia … Mangia … Mangia …

WE ARE ALL ALIVE
AT THE SAME TIME
HURTLING THROUGH SPACE

Written in Portlaoise

'NOT IN BLOCK CAPITALS like that, they look too confrontational. Like a row of burly American footballers with warpaint on their faces all staring *you* down like a hungry tiger would see you, as a spindly little chicken drumstick, Christ! Put some weight on, Louis, and that's an order from the prime minister.'

She jabs her skinny attaché, genuinely wondering where he puts those big roast dinners, which she pays for, that she sees him eat on Sundays after they've woken up and spent the morning fucking.

He blushes and clears his throat. 'Ahem.'

A little quirk he must have picked up from his father, she thinks. 'Genetic' behaviour? Nonsense. Nurture. These things are passed down like family heirlooms. That little throat-clearing probably survived at least two or three world wars. But he doesn't know. He doesn't know much about himself; most people don't know much about themselves at all.

'Ahem. Ahem,' she coughs, mimicking him, making fun.

After they make love on his grisly bed, she asks Louis about the youth. She says, what are you people like? What do you like? Definitely not me. What makes you tick? What's it like inside the brain of a young person who's never existed without the assistance of a mobile phone? What does that do to the mind?

Why, she thinks, do I feel such a gulf between me and most, no all (bar Louis) young people I speak to? I feel like an alien visiting from another planet.

He can't answer, because he doesn't know himself. Being young must be being fine with not knowing, she thinks. Some live until they're ninety-five and don't know, so haven't really grown old at all, only physically.

Louis follows his little throat ahem with words – 'Now, stop it, PM. No dilly-dallying. We have exactly zero time left.'

Aha, so there *is* a compulsion to the little throat-clearing, it wasn't just a tickly throat. That is, *of course*, why he inherited it from his father, she thinks. Because his old man used it to preface an order barked at young Louis, and so, in it went into the young rake's brain and lodged itself. It is his father – the ripple of him, anyway, and probably his father before him, and on and on until God knows when. 'So, Louis has just ordered *me*, the top dog, to stop prattling on and get back to the task at hand, chop chop! Oh God, how that turns me on.'

Maybe, she thinks, *that's* why we began fucking in the first place – that little throat tic. It must make me feel like someone else is in charge for a change and have only now just realised it. Ha. So, in a sense, I'm not sleeping with this young whippersnapper, I'm actually sleeping with his father. Sleeping with a man I've never met. Maybe I'll add that into the list of achievements in my memoir.

'You're right, boss. This lettering is a bit bullish,' he says.

'Exactly, Louis. We don't want to scare them. Not with this one, anyway,' she says.

'How about something a little more delicate? Perhaps a rather subtle italic-style print?' he says.

She smiles at him. 'Yes. Oh, Louis.' She leans forward so he can see right down into the groove of her cleavage. A cleavage that has seen better days, when it was a liver-spotless cleavage, but that was at least twenty years ago. 'You always know how to hit the nail right on the head.' And she licks her lips, but she's only about two-thirds around the rim of her mouth with her tongue when another attaché comes in, Perry. Who's a right gossip and a git, and walked into Number 10 because of his uncle. Talentless, brainless little twerp. She manages to recover herself from the sexy lip-rimming before Perry sees, or so she hopes.

'What is it, Perry?' she says.

'All world leaders are in their seats, Madam. The press are in place. They are ready for you, ready for the big global transmission!' Perry sort of raises his arms in a limp attempt to express excitement, but it looks more like someone just defibrillated him between the shoulder blades.

'Thank you, Perry.'

'I've got it!' Louis rejoices. 'The correct print for the background. You are going to love it.'

Oh, she does love when he tells her what she's going to feel. Do. Not Do. Create. Destroy. Leave. Stay, because, you know –

Out she steps out onto the podium to face the world, with the enormous, yet delicate, lettering dwarfing her beneath –

WE ARE ALL ALIVE
AT THE SAME TIME
HURTLING THROUGH SPACE

Flash, flash, flash. Silence, for a while. She clears her throat. 'Ahem.'

SALVADOR DALY

Written (mostly) in Los Angeles

I KNEW THIS FELLA in the home town. He couldn't paint but he was a fire bug – a proper little pyromaniac.

Cling! Cling! you'd hear his Zippo go. *Cling! Cling!* early in the morning.

Night's close and he'd be up before the cock crows in the summertime, roaming through the parish, ears perked for a clock to spoil his silence. And when he heard the alarm going off – *cling!* – he'd be in that bedroom window and on it with the Zippo.

Mad coincidence, really, him and the artist fella having such similar names and such similar dislike for clocks.

Mam says he'd keep us all punctual, would Salvador – at least we've that to be grateful for. I says, yah, and grateful for another one of God's mysteries – that he hasn't been banged up for manslaughter.

He'd the whole town trained well enough, to wake up *seconds* before their alarm. Jesus forgive me, you'd be raging when you'd beat the clock with waking by two minutes. Or one minute. Or ten seconds … Leaping out of your skin from sleep – *CLING!* – where you'd have dreamt the flames.

If Daly was round your house, he'd melt anything he found around trying to tell you the time. To the point where he wouldn't try to hide it, like. The clock went off and me in the shower once and I didn't hear. I came back in to find the whole bedstead and the head-board all charred and blackened. But the alarm on it still worked for ages.

And in school – writhing around or passed out in the desk. The nuns never let him sit at the back anywhere near the coats. He full emptied himself in Brennan's class once, woke up and didn't give a bollocks. Didn't even go to the toilet. It stank. It made my eyes water.

It was around that time he stayed up in Butcho's on some kind of social respite thing during the big trial, till they cleared Fergal. And the rest. But no one knows for sure, all sworn to secrecy. Butcho came downstairs one morning and Salvador was using printer paper to set the old grandfather clock alight. Belonged to Butcho's grandad, was in the family for ages and never told the right time. Butcho had to chase him out into the garden with pots and pans, where Salvador had burnt circles into their lawn of grass.

And Butcho told me Salvador'd bars of chocolate stashed out in the tool shed and in under the hedges.

All over the place. He found a pound of Kerrygold once hid way up the rowan red-berry tree.

Butcho's cousin Kev lives about a twenty-five-euro taxi out past Butcho in the sticks, and he said stumbling in at the end of the night he saw Salvador out there, alone in the field. Cartwheeling, cheering, celebrating something Kev couldn't see. Kev's father had to go out with the shotgun once or twice, but gave him a fair wide berth. Salvador would've built camps out in the ditch, sure. He stayed out there days, apparently. He'd eat the grass out of the ground, letting off bangers and howling at the moon.

And always burning black circles – into the grass on the green, into Butcho's fields after they'd the wheat cut. Permanent marker painting them all big and small onto people's walls. Some kind of weird calling-card thing, like the Joker. But Butcho put a stop to it when he was living round theirs, anyway, by drawing clock faces inside them! All it took was the twelve and the six to send Salvador into fits.

Then, in the church – was it one of them Noonans who was doing more of the devil's work in God's house? Moss Noonan, I think, the second one, snuck up the aisle that Christmas Eve, almost halfway, to tell Salvador that the pointy thing made of stone behind Father Banville, at the foot of Jesus Christ Almighty, was in fact a sundial. Lads used them for telling the time back in Bible days. Moss Noonan whispering, and he hunkered down low in the aisle in mock prayer.

Salvador gets up, calm as Christmas, and saunters up the aisle. You'd always know he was near by the stink of piss and petrol. Straight up past Banville at the podium, who pulls the aul' ostrich tactics. Banville, about to leap out of his robes but keeps the show going. Salvador walks right up on to the altar – on the busiest night of the whole year! – in his red-and-black tracksuit, all oily patches. Sinister. Like the devil. Always plagued with nose bleeds under the cowboy hat he'd have got in Gorta, dark brown and broken down.

Out comes his tin of lighter fluid anyway, and he squirts expert all over the sundial, splashing Jesus's shins, splashing Jesus's poor bloodied feet and he hanging on the cross, heaven forgive us, then out with the Zippo. *Cling!* Woof.

I've never seen a priest move so fast – and it Banville's big night. Aw! Altar Banville was just Smoke Banville, like from Looney Tunes. A flash of the white and gold robes and he gone, out into the carpark.

All filing out after, with Salvador there on the altar, roaring. Doubled over in tears. Lit by the blaze. Putting it true, God lifted him from somewhere and could find nowhere, so put him here instead to torment us.

But it was all right in the end. Bit of craic. Kinda biblical. Banville refound his rhythm when all the flashing lights showed up – the blues and all the reds. They managed to get in and douse it before the manger went up. Moss was looking a bit hot under the collar as Banville climbed up on the back of Gerraghty's Elantra and finished off the Mass to great cheer. Then he was up to Doheny's drinking free pints, cocking a flirt. He wasn't letting his big night get burned down.

They'd to cuff Salvador to get him out past the Mass, the poor misfortunate, roaring and screeching. Flapping around like a ferret. Them thick eyebrows of his singed off him for the umpteenth time.

Fergal following him out behind. With the bright red head on him. Chatting to the guards. Used to the routine, I suppose. Grinning at everyone, like it's a great laugh. Flushed. Peaky looking. Always looks like he's about to spontaneously combust, does Fergal. And the guard with the hat on behind him looked guilty carrying the tin of lighter fluid.

The church did a whip round then, to sit Salvador down with some kind of therapist. I said, 'Mam, is that where the church's money could do the most good? What about the millions of black babies with flyblown eyes and river blindness and all that in Africa, and they sitting Salvador down in some posh office full of expensive furniture? It's a tinderbox.'

She said to me, 'Mark, remind yourself to thank God that there's people like young Salvador Daly in the world to remind the rest of us that we're better off. Sure, how else would we know?' Yah, right …

A few years later, he went up then for some burning offence or another. We didn't see him for ages. We were twelve, thirteen by that point. Was it when he did Gerraghty's up at the end of the estate's hedges? Yah, must've been. Right around the whole house – imagine. And Tony up doing the guttering. He stayed up there and called the wife to ring the guards, and they dragged Salvador off and he screaming, 'They're already dead, they're already dead!' So they say.

He did a fair whack of damage that time. Folks got worried then, so charges was finally brought. Not before time. Even Mam said it was just. To tangle the Dalys back up in the Dublin courts raked up a lot of ill feeling in the town, but it had to be done. There was fair tension. No one wanted to talk about it, but everyone wanted to talk about it. Only human. And Banville was even gaslighting us all on it via the sermon. Up to Dublin Salvador was sent anyway.

Behind Her Honour in the court was one of them big red digital readouts – just for telling what time had passed in the proceedings, like. But Salvador wasn't having any of it. Fergal told whatshername who lives the street opposite not a minute had passed before Salvador flicked a match and sent it sailing clean over the judge's head. Missed her wig by a small inch. And he'd five or six lit and flicked before he was dragged out again and thrown in the cage, crying laughing.

After, though, Butcho's cousin was saying down Doheny's it wasn't a judge he was flicking fire at at all, that there was no charges brought, it wasn't for that – that she was some social-services thing to do with the Dalys' first merry-go-round in the Dublin courts. When the whole town put his mother's tragedy on trial, he wasn't even ten years old by that point – he was a year less than me. Who knows whose floorboards she ended up under! God forgive us. But the longer the case went on, the more it was like Cluedo. Not just the milkman, but half the men of the town summoned for questioning. Proof of time and place, please, sir. The joke down in Doheny's was, was it Tony Gerraghty with the wrench in the ballroom? Was it the dusky milkman with the candlestick in the billiard room? Was it Father Banville with the gold chalice in the vestry?! Or was it Salvador, with his mother's own alpine cuckoo clock? And so on …

But Butcho's a slow burn. He'd be a terror for sticking the boot in a bit too far. Sometimes. On a smoke break outside Doheny's, pulling passing legs, he'd see Fergal, flapping like a *Golden Pages* down the main street – in the textbook high-volume shell suit, grinning, in case anyone had a pop.

'Here, Fergal! It's a fire warning label they should've stitched onto that young lad of yours down the orphanage.'

'Ha! Sunny day,' says Fergal, and points at the sky. 'That's all the clock I need – he can't burn that!'

Butcho, pullin' on the last of a fag – 'Good man.'

Big wave off of Fergal as his head goes like a cherry tomato. And hair like a tomato's little green crop as well.

He was always peaky looking, even in full health. Even in the height of summer.

See, Salvador was a swarthy young fellow. Head of curls, and eyebrows when they weren't singed off. Like a crusty Spanish pirate. Wouldn't be shocking looking, now, after a good going over with the shears. If he'd only wash …

It seemed the only common trait Salvador and his father Fergal had was they both looked like they were going to spontaneously combust. For different reasons.

It was common knowledge, of course it was, around the parish.

Comments were often fired at young Salvador too – only a bit of leg pulling. Sure, we all got it for something.

After that Christmas Eve Mass catastrophe of '96, it took a small fortune to conclude that Salvador's clock destruction all stemmed from a lot of repressed anger due to the fact he was clearly a product of the dusky milkman and not Fergal. 'Big whoop,' I said to Mam. 'We needed a mirror, not a counsellor to tell us that.'

And he wasn't half-punctual, that milkman. Impeccable timekeeping. You could set your watch by him. He was reliable to the point where people didn't mind him.

He was ex-military, you see. The way the lads'd be telling it is funny, but he was some kinda reckless sort of maverick back in the day. Not unlike a certain young Salvador. He stole a tank drunk one night and went cruising miles from the barracks on a promise. Then early the following morning, he'd gone and left it parked sideways in the officers' quarters parking, across a space clearly labelled COMMANDANT. And it was well known that this commandant's temper was liable to swell to nuclear-strike levels. The base's alarm was signalled and the men were all woken up, and this commandant proceeds to lose his almighty shit in his pyjamas. The arses were run off the men till they were delirious and sick. Day in, day out, they ran till they puked. And resentments grew – Jesus forgive me, of course they would – until the dusky milkman's given name (unknown) was eventually muttered in the commandant's ear.

That was it – he got the boot. Dishonourable discharge. He took it on the chin and left quietly, I heard. And ended up traded in cruising a tank for cruising a milk float. Delivering bottles of milk and more besides! Might've been one of them spin-the-globe-type jobs because who knows what ties he has or what ties he's cut. Ending up there, ending up here … Mam says the Lord works in mysterious ways, *mar dhea*.

Like poor Salvador's mother, who remains a mystery to this day. Nicola, may she rest, God bless her. Terrible shame. She'd a great brightness and a fine shine off her. Tall and blonde and built like an Olympic swimmer.

Reports were she was up every morning before the first cuckoo on the clock, and Salvador watching morning cartoons. She'd be looking out the window, wringing her hands. Checking her complexion in the mirror, checking for flecks of red on her teeth. Oh, I bet. God forgive us … *Gong. Cuckoo!* Six o'clock on the dot would announce his float, motoring up the road. Cruising along, with the milk bottles clinking.

After Salvador's round of posh therapy sessions, anyway, it was decreed that the best thing for him was distraction. Mam came home from church group one evening quacking one of Banville's turns of phrase: 'We've to give him something to replace the fire!' So we thought, start him off with something small. Make deals that are reward based, that kind of thing.

So, to scupper his usual morning routine he was given another. A paper round. Sounded good on paper … He'd have a few quid in his pocket. He might even take up personal hygiene as a hobby. We didn't get our hopes up. All under one proviso: no Zippo. I was told 'shut up, Mark' when I remarked how those would be instructions for Salvador to ignore. Despite my advisement, he was brought in and sat down with the group, given a cup of tea, and the plan was put to him. He was fairly blank-looking at first, till he heard the word money. And then he shrugged an OK. So, we were hopeful.

Little did we know how much shit, God ignore me, he was due to fire at the fan.

I must say, though, that the eve of Salvador's paper round was probably the best night's sleep this town has ever had – knowing the morning didn't have him roaming around, ears pricked. But not me. And Mammy will attest. I'm not one to say I told you so, but I knew well he'd find a way to destroy a good thing.

The town is a glorified crossroads. Just after dawn, Caroline Shaw saw – she lives there above the solicitor's, peeping out her lace curtains. She'd be always down Doheny's declaring she's owed free drink because she was the first to call it in. You'd hear her whining on to Butcho. But Butcho'd fair quieten her by saying, 'Well, what were you doing awake at that time anyway, Caroline, peeping through your lacy curtains?' And she'd give him a fair dose of the I'll-murder-you eyes. He'd be holding his own, all right, but he'd be liable to go red as Fergal. I often wondered, d'you know, if there wasn't some little thing going on between her and Butcho, and he nearly twenty years her junior. Sure, the devil works through her too. She'd have half the town rode, God forgive us, and that wouldn't take long.

The morning of Daly's paper round anyway, regular as the seasons, the dusky milkman rumbles over the horizon of the road into town – 6.24 a.m. on the spot, I was told.

Which, goes without saying, would've given him ample time up in Dalys' back in the day. Out in the converted shed, and Fergal asleep in bed? God forgive us. But not Salvador …

Anyway, 6.24 a.m. The rumbling of the float clinking with bottles could already be heard coming over the hill. And Salvador was stood below, as tall as his full height would muster. Right in the middle of the junction. Waiting. Standing. With the cowboy hat on he'd have got down in Gorta. And a golden sheriff's badge on, pinned to his black-and-red oily tracksuit, which was all stuffed with bits of balled-up newspapers. He had them stuffed into his pockets, into his elastic waistband of his tracksuit bottoms, into his socks and his shoes. He'd even a newspaper in his teeth, Caroline said.

The float rumbles to a halt 'bout twenty feet in front of Salvador the gaucho. The milkman gets out of the float and kills the engine. And they both stand there. Eyes locked. Nothing being said. Take Salvador, now, to disrupt the dusky milkman's impeccable timekeeping.

Caroline said it was like the Bad and the Ugly, and the Good was on his lunchbreak! Or still asleep

– something like that. She tells it brilliant. A while goes by, anyway, neither one making a move. With the float's engine dead, the scene is dead silent. Just the cawing of the crows egging them on.

I thought Salvador'd go for him but, no – in a rare move, he *clings* that bastard Zippo, bends down and lights up the newspapers all stashed in his clothes. *Woof!* What a rare boy.

She said she never seen a milkman move so fast but the flames moved quicker. Salvador'd likely pre-doused himself. Caroline said you could hear him laughing. He shrivelled down to his hunkers but his arms were still in the air – cheering something, celebrating something. Something Caroline couldn't see.

At lightning speed, the milkman whips the lids off two bottles, hurries over and douses the milk over Salvador's head. Big white fountains of the stuff pouring down on top of burning Salvador.

Frozen in that Nixon pose – with the hands in the air after he won the election, or after he got kicked out – the black and the red all melted into him. The milkman gathers Salvador up quick in his coat and drives him himself the four miles to the hospital, quick as the float can carry them. He wasn't delivering nothing that morning, only Salvador …

Caroline ran up the road to the police station in her bathrobe. In she went, roaring into reception, and she said the guard looked weary when he'd to put down his bacon sandwich.

I'm told there was an interest took in Salvador after that by the dusky milkman. Mam said it's about time.

I'd say they must've mistaken him for a foreign doctor going in visiting the hospital in the big white coat!

I tell you what, though, you wouldn't catch me roaring it from our rooftop, but Mam was right, after all. These days … things get quare dead with no Salvador around. No little devil keeping us on our toes – *Cling! Cling!* – to remind us how good we really are.

He has a kid now, I heard … Salvador. By some wan he met in the army. Think he's a welder of some kind now as well. But the deep underwater kind of welding, the shit you get paid serious money for. Salvador in a scuba suit – oh, the irony. Haven't seen him around here for years …

GERTIE CRONIN: MEMORIES OF A YOUNG GUARD

by Joseph Sheehan

Written in Donoghue's Pub, Portlaoise

GO UP SUNDAY THEN for the dinner and the tea in the evening to Gertie. 'Twas o'erlooking the whole of Cork city, this house. And she was … The food was grand. 'Twas three pound a week, three old punts, old pounds, before the punt or the euro or anything. And a pound for the station.

Gertie was great craic. We weren't lodging – she'd just make the dinner and the tea in the evening. That was for about five of us. Jaysus, little dining room, lovely now, jaysus, picturesque, and then she'd bring in the food and 'twas grand, sure.

But she was a great character, though. She'd stand at the window. Do you know, you'd get the message too if you listened, do you see, you know, rather than mouthing, thinking you were an expert at that age.

She'd say, 'I remember looking out the window, boy, and the fuckin' Tans were burning the city, and the fuckin' auxiliaries. They burned the city,' she says, 'from St Luke's down to the Town Hall.' After the Kilmichael ambush – she saw it, you see.

And it'd kind of garner you a bit of respect for the woman, even as a young fella. I think it was around nineteen – when Kilmichael happened – around nineteen twenty, twenty-one. They wrote off the auxiliaries over there. Then they came back into the city and burned the city, you see.

She was a little peteen of a woman, ah, and tough as fuck. She was a lovely woman, God almighty. It was only no distance from the station, and that'd close between six and seven. Up to Gertie for the tea. She was lovely, she was feckin' great.

She'd have a sister then, Bina. And she couldn't cook for worth of shit. Aw, she'd poison you, boy. When Gertie'd be gone off, jaysus, you'd be left with Bina. B–I–N–A. Never heard it.

We were used to toughness, like. Gertie was a lovely aul' lady. She was a real mother hen. She had a sort understanding with the station above. She'd provide the grub.

And Buckley, that same Buckley who went off and got married and went off with himself. Who had me accuse the aul' lad on the bike for having no light or a reflector. This aul' fella, on a bike. I can still picture him. 'Whaaa?!' Haha! And I'd say he said to himself, 'This is some gobshite now.' Nah, and he on a bike and not a light – I'd say it hadn't a light on it in the last forty years.

The thing was, d'you see, I was kind of wondering to myself, I better get a few summonses. You know? Because they'll say I'm doing nothing, which I suppose would be technically right. There was no such thing as a quota, but if you were doing something, surely to God, like, you'd come across some offences somewhere, traffic offences, you know. If I had nothing at all, they'd say, jaysus this fella isn't doing nothing, and they'd be right about that, like.

You're bound to, you know ... But I says, and yer man, of course, smart arse from Clare, the fella Buckley with me, he says, 'Sure, look at yer man on the bike comin' there now, sure,' he said.

Now, summonsing an aul' fella on a bike in nine-teen-seventy-three down in Cork on an auld high Nelly black bike – ha – wouldn't have been the most serious offence under the traffic law that you ever came across, like, he knowing well. It hadn't happened in Cork, I'd say, for years, like, you know, because they'd give out to them but there'd be no summonses, like. And if you ended up over in court with it – if you were stupid enough to summons him for having no front light, back light and no rear reflector and went into court with it, you'd be the laughing stock of the city, like. You know, so yer man Buckley was actually setting me up, makin' an eejit out of me.

For god's sake, like, you'd just say to yer man, 'Look, if I see you again I'll definitely, you'll definitely get a summons,' and give out, like, and blah blah. Jaysus, to go to that extreme. An aul' lad, d'you know, on his aul' bike.

Jim Buckley. Chrisht, don't put him in the book now, don't put his name in it – he's still around, like. He mightn't be too impressed with his name clomped in the book. He was from Clare, just. Ah, he was a – he used to mind us, you know, used to be out with him, you know, he was in charge of me, like, sort of. He was supposed to be teaching me. Teaching me, all right. Setting me up to make a fool out of me.

Like, when you're nineteen years of age, like, you'd be a small biteen gullible. You learn quick, like. These fellas wouldn't be behind the door about putting you in a dilemma that you'd have a job of getting yourself out of. And a big laugh.

They sent me up Grá na Bráthair one time then on dog licences. D'you see, because there wasn't a whole lot happening. Dog licences? You'd as much chance of getting … You had to get an owner for the dog. You'd as much chance, now, of getting an owner for a dog back then up in Grá na Bráthair as I have of becoming the next pope. The dog could be inside changing the television with the remote control, and yer man, 'He's not mine at all – I dunno where he came from, boy.' Ah, jays, I copped on after an hour, I says fuck this now, boys below having a great fuckin' laugh sending the young fella up, d'you see.

But you didn't put a uniform on just to be some sort of an authoritarian gobshite goin' round. And the job can attract that type a certain amount. It does without a doubt, yeah, they can be a feckin' pain. And then they try and get themselves promoted, and they get themselves promoted on people's backs, and their colleagues' backs.

Gertie was telling me one day … I'd say I got to kind of like Gertie – we used to have great chats. She said, 'When the Tans were around, d'you see, there was a curfew. Everyone had to be inside.' Oh yeah, at that time in the city – eight o' clock, you wouldn't come out, and you didn't.

There was this character. Jays, he was an awful one for the beer. And he'd go into the pubs on Blarney Street, and the pubs would be open but, no, you couldn't go out the door, like. They'd be patrolling the streets, you know? He used to, he'd come up … Blarney Street, past her backyard. You could hear him, she said. And he'd be well drunk, wherever he'd get the drink. Coming up Blarney Street, they'd be patrolling up and down, and he'd start singing at the top of his voice and the whole fuckin' street would hear him.

'To Cairo Sam! You are undone!' Be roaring this out. 'You better give the Maxim gun. The bhoys of Munster will show *you* fun! On the lonely road to Bandon.'

When they moved out of the city, d'you see. Taunting them with 'The Lonely Road to Bandon', that if they moved out towards West Cork they were fucked, like, which they were. There's no doubt that he wasn't exaggerating.

Then all you hear is, 'Fuck off home, Paddy!'

But they never did a thing to him. Never did a thing. Got so used to him that, that they thought, 'Ah, fuckin eejit, leave him alone.'

Weren't all bad really. Bad enough though.

Gertie used say, 'It's great to see such grand young lads wearing such nice uniforms, instead of them bastards with their funny accents.'

Ha! You see, we were one of her own. They could be fighting with us, arguing with us, but this is what we fought for.

Right. Right, rock and roll.

[Drinks the end of the pint of Guinness.]

ACKNOWLEDGEMENTS

I want to show my gratitude to as many as I can remember to thank. If I read you a rough something and your name isn't on here, I'm sorry. It's only a failing of my memory. To the ones who gave me their ears …

Firstly, Gill Books – for taking a leap of faith with me. It was bold and brave of you, and for that I'm very grateful.

Catherine Gough, the perpetually patient and encouraging editor.

Emma Dunne for such sound advice.

Conor Nagle for valuable encouragement early on.

Rose Parkinson and Faith O'Grady for being a bedrock of support and useful insight.

Joe Sheehan, for secreting song and verse as the tongue secretes saliva.

Patrick McCabe for giving me his precious time and approval.

Dinesh Ramachandran for showing me the power of the stories I tell myself inside my head.

To Maria Sheehan, Ari Gold, Jessica Thomas, Sasha Penco, Tim Digby-Bell, Bonnie Wong, Emel Michael, Shane Booth, Irina Lytchak, Cameron Britton, David Castañeda, Eliyah Sekulova – for being potent creative forces in your own right, and for giving me that rare gift one person can give to another: listening.